ENRULE

Not all those who wander
are Lost!

HOLLY SPARKS

Editing by Jill Weinstein
Cover Art by Jessica Allain
Formatted by Champagne Formats

ISBN-13: 978-1519542946

ISBN-10: 1519542941

For my family, who has always believed in me.
But when zombies really do take over, in order to survive, I'd only have to outrun all of YOU!!!

Hehe.

There's a greater evil than monsters.

Chapter 1

I NEVER KNEW IT COULD hurt this much, having your life torn apart. Watching everything you love burn to ashes. The ones that kept you sane…gone. The haunting memories of the past replay in my mind, over and over until I want to throw up. I never thought something like this could happen. Nor did I ever think the world could feel this way. Dark, empty and alone. Nightmares flash by with every second that I'm still breathing. I don't know how I've survived this long — I guess I've changed. Somehow I've adjusted myself to react to danger, to the most horrific dreams imaginable. The world isn't what it used to be, nor will it ever be the same again. My name is Ella, and this is my story.

"You, in here!"

Loud, unbearable gunfire goes off to my far left but I keep

walking. The damp metal ground beneath me echoes down the enclosed tunnel with every step. The steel walls block us from the outside world. I, and so many other survivors, all walk together. Some huddle up to each other, afraid of what is next. *I am too*, I think to myself.

The light above us flickers on and off as the damp water drips from the ceiling. A rotten, musty smell fills the air surrounding us. Boys and girls from all ages walk alongside me, all with the same expression. Emptiness. My messed-up mind gets thrown back into the awful memories that are sketched into my soul. My heart aches, like broken jagged pieces have been ripped out of me all at once. It beats slowly while I silently listen to its rhythm. My whole body feels torn and beaten, as if there is no point going on in this dreadful world any longer.

A numbness is all I feel, taking over my whole body. My mind tries to process what's happening, but my head feels blurry with the loss of my family. My loved ones. Gone. As my hands start to tremble, a single tear falls down my cold cheeks. I close my eyes. The pain takes over, creating a protective wall around the silent beat of my heart, protecting it from any more agony. Any more hurt.

"I said YOU!" A finger aims at me as one of the terrifying soldiers points toward a room on our right. The curved walls are at least fifteen-feet high and there is a large, dome-shaped door the solider points to. "In here." The slimy grin on his face widens when I look up at him with wary eyes.

I walk toward the soldier in front of the group. He wears all black and carries a huge machine gun. Glaring at me, he pushes his strong hand against my back. My body feels weak and fragile, as if it could break at any second. As he shoves me, I go flying head first through the doorway. We are brought here for our own safety, and this is what happens? I couldn't feel more alone in my life.

Before me is a large room filled with single, metal beds on the left and right. The curved walls are dark grey, reflecting my inner emotions. They join at the tip of the ceiling, forming a point. About fifty beds are lined up against the two walls, with only a small width between them. Metal bedposts and tiny blankets are all that we have at the moment, which terrifies me on its own. *What little we have will soon be gone...and then what?*

When I look down, I see that the ground is stained with dirty footprints. The smell of sweat suddenly finds its way into my senses, causing me to shiver.

"Move!" The soldier pushes me again and I stumble forward.

The heat inside me starts to boil up at the way I'm being treated. I look up and take a clearer look around the place. *Surely they must have the wrong room.* The room is filled with boys, boys from all age groups, Most of them appear to be in their late teens to early twenties.

They all whip their heads around, looking at me. I suddenly feel self-conscious, clutching the pair of spare clothes I was given. Most of them look shocked to have a girl walk in whilst they are changing. Then there are the others who look me up and down, grinning. *Ugh.* They have obviously lived here for a quite a while, judging by how relaxed they all seem.

I soon blank them all out. Nothing can mend the hole in my crushed soul. The sacrifices my family have made for me is the only thing keeping me going. The horrific memories shatter my heart once again as they pull at the broken pieces of my spirit. I quickly turn around to ask the soldier if he has the right room but the metal door slams in my face. My heart beats quicker as I turn around, facing them all.

A tall guy on my left smiles at me. "Alright there, darling?" I ignore him as I make my way into the room, looking for a spare bed.

A group of guys on my left taunt me. "You can share mine if

ya want?" Tears start to pour down my face as I wipe them away. I hurry down the room quickly to get away from the sneers, trying desperately to block out this nightmare.

Another guy walks by me. "Why do you look so frightened, girly?" I shove past him as I walk over the stained floor in search of an empty bed. A group sits to my right, looking a little sorry for me as they continue to get changed. They were obviously not expecting female company.

I finally find a bed in the middle of the dormitory. The room holds at least fifty people and I seem to be the only girl. It doesn't matter to me since being in a room full of girls wouldn't make much difference. I place the spare clothes on the bed and inhale a deep breath. *How do I get changed in here? Surely they have a bathroom or something.* I need to get these clothes off me. The torn and battered jeans I wear just remind me of the attack.

"Afraid of getting changed in front of a load of guys?" A boy to my left sits on the bed next to mine. He has shaggy brown hair and intriguing bright, blue eyes. He wears all leather, same as everyone else. He smiles at me as I look down at my new clothes once again. I take the pin out of my blonde hair and let my ponytail fall down my back. Next, I take off my jacket and place it on the bed.

"Look, boys! She's getting changed," a guy down the room shouts out. I sigh when my eyes start to well up again. I think about what I have lost, and why I ever thought that this was the best place to go to survive.

"What are you waiting for?" the boy next to me says, shooting me an accusing look. His blue eyes lock with mine and I shiver under his slimy watch. I shake my head and ignore him.

"There's a bathroom down at the end," A deep voice comes from behind me. I look around and a pair of golden brown eyes meet mine. He looks me up and down before turning around to finish unpacking his things. His short brown hair is still damp and his rippling muscles bulge through his short sleeves.

"Thank you," I respond quietly. He doesn't acknowledge me any further. Picking up my clothes, I walk down through the dorm quickly, ignoring all the catcalls and vulgar comments getting thrown at me. Finally I reach what looks to be a bathroom.

I stand in the doorway while I peer inside. The room is massive, with at least ten showerheads on the wall. No privacy at all. There are a few stalls at the back with toilets in them, but they have no door. *Just great.* Walking back to my bed, I sigh. I'll just have to suck it up. I'm lucky to be alive and I'm afraid of getting changed in front of these guys? *No.* I've got to be brave from now on. Taking off my damp bloodstained clothes, I try to cover myself up as best I can. I can feel eyes watching me from around the room, but I no longer care.

The guy on my left winks. "Come on, girly. We're all friends in here." *Ugh.*

I quickly change into the pair of black leather trousers, and a small black top that clings to my skin. I hear whistling being aimed at me but I choose to ignore it. I look to my right, but the boy who helped me is gone, leaving his clothes on the bed.

A speaker goes off above us all. "ALL NEW SURVIVORS TO THE REP HALL."

"Where's the Rep Hall?" I ask the guy on my left, who is still smirking at me.

"Down the main tunnel," he answers, giving my body a once-over. "Looking good." He smiles yet again and his blue eyes sparkle with amusement.

I take a deep breath and walk down the room, heading for the door.

Chapter 2

I PUSH THE DOOR OPEN to exit the dorm, and step into the hallway. Other new survivors walk past me, just as confused with their new surroundings as I am. Following them, we all finally come to another large door in front of us. It opens with ease and we all crowd into the one room. It's massive. The ceiling is at least two stories high and the walls are dark, with a few flamed torches dotted around the room. The place is alive with conversation and light.

"Our new survivors. Welcome." A man steps out of the shadows and faces us. He holds out his arms, welcoming us all. He looks like he's in his late thirties. He has a few grey hairs and hypnotising, dark blue eyes. I can see the slight creases in his forehead from where he's been scowling. The dark leather outfit is clinging to his strong build, and as I look closer I can see a rather distinctive tattoo on his right arm. The dark black circle surrounds a letter. I squint my eyes to see the tattoo closer but he turns away from me.

"Welcome to the Underground. Here you will learn basic defence and attacks to keep you safe for when we return to the world above."

A few more people have joined the group, which makes up about thirty of us. I think most of us came from the same little town but I can't be sure. When the pickup truck came to collect us, I don't remember seeing this many people alive.

"I'm Derrick. I'm in charge of the many survivors we hold here. I will teach you how to defend yourselves and how to survive. We need as many of you as possible to cooperate with our system. There are many survivors out there and we need to help them. Without learning the basic defences, you don't stand a chance." He raises his chin higher in the air to seem more intimidating, but he doesn't scare me. "Our leaders will train you into soldiers. The training will be hard, tough, and many of you will fail. Those who don't possess the skills of a soldier will be assigned other duties, such as cooking, cleaning, and guarding the wall. Others will show exemplary skills, and those of you with the courage and bravery will venture out into the unknown, rescuing others."

If people need help out there, then I will do what I can. I can't let what happened to me happen to any more innocent lives out there.

Derrick talks about the Underground for another half an hour explaining the rules and regulations here. Most of them just repeat themselves over and over.

Rules of the Underground:

1. No survivors are to wander out of their allocated dormitory at any time on their own.
2. If over the age of 12 you must report for training every morning. Exceptions include: illness, injuries, etc.

> 3. Anyone who leaves the Underground without permission will be considered lost. We cannot be responsible for anyone on the outside.
> 4. Meals will be served in the Rep Hall. Rations are low and will be served twice a day.
> 5. After exactly ten weeks of training, you will be sent out to look for new survivors, accompanying our loyal soldiers.

Ten weeks? That's too long!

"People are depending on you. Do not let us down!" Derrick stands proud.

How are we supposed to save more lives if we are cooped up in here for a whole ten weeks?

"Defence starts in the morning. You will meet your leader in the training room." His voice echoes as he walks back into the shadows. Through the darkness I see a slight scar slithering up his face, under his right eye. It's silvery and shines in the moonlight. *How odd.*

I look around at the other survivors. A man and a woman stand next to me. Their eyes are filled with love for each other. It makes me think back to what I have lost. My parents. My sister. My brother. My whole family. The disturbing scene plays back in my head. The way they were taken from me. The whole town screaming. Fires burning. Hell-raising. I have to stay strong. I can't break down — I won't let myself.

A girl walks next to me as I make my way down the tunnel. She looks about nineteen…my age. Her long brown hair is pulled back in a ponytail and she wears a sparkling nose stud. Her green eyes glisten in the flickering lights above us as she turns around to face me.

"Kira." She nods.

I return her nod. "Ella."

She narrows her eyes at me.

"You'll have to work on those muscles of yours, you know," she says, looking ahead at the tunnel, wearing a slightly amused expression. "They won't let a scrawny thing like you out there." She then nods at me again and walks off ahead.

I look down at my body and sigh. Maybe she's right. Maybe I don't have what it takes, but I sure as hell want to protect every other living survivor out there! Returning to my dorm, I hurry through the tall metal door. I feel as if all eyes are on me. *Not this again.*

"You alright, sweetheart?" A boy comes up to me.

"I'm fine." I budge past him and ignore all the eyes that bore into me. My heart still aches, trying to recover from the hole that's burnt into it, but I use the hurt I feel and turn it into strength.

"We got ourselves a feisty one here, lads!" Another guy laughs and a few others join in. Sitting on my bed, I look at the boys on the opposite side of the room. They seem to be harmless, just talking amongst themselves. They seem different than the others. Slowly, I start to walk over to them. One boy with dark black hair and blue eyes sees me walking over and all three of them look up.

"Do you mind if I sit?" I say, gesturing to one of the beds.

"No, of course." The dark-haired boy shuffles over a little to give me more room.

"How are you finding it here?" Another says, looking at me.

"Okay," I lie, with a forced smile.

"I'm Jim." The dark-haired boy shakes my hand. "This is Terry and George." He gestures to the other two boys. They both have mousey brown hair and green eyes. They both shake my hand also.

"I'm sorry you got stuck with all the guys," George says, tilting his head slightly in sympathy.

"It's no big deal," I say, with a shrug.

"Where do ya come from?" Jim asks.

"Redcross." I reply. They all nod, knowing the same thing. There weren't many survivors from there, so they don't say much more.

"I'm Ella."

"Nice to meet you, Ella," Terry says. He smiles at me in a comforting way.

Talking amongst ourselves for a little while, I learn that Jim and his three sisters had come here. Terry's parents are still out there, waiting to be rescued. They had all come from little towns like mine, with an equal amount of survivors. George has no one. His whole family is gone. He feels what I'm feeling, I can tell.

Looking back over to the other side of the dorm, the boy I'd seen earlier returns to his bed next to mine. He lifts a few wooden crates and carries them over to the other side of the room. He stacks them against the metal wall. He seems slightly older than the others but still quite young. His tanned skin and his muscular arms flex as he carries the large crates. He looks over and catches me gazing at him. I quickly divert my eyes and dive right back into the conversation going on amongst our little group.

Suddenly the bell starts to go off above us, interrupting our conversation. Most of the boys start to get changed as they climb into bed.

"That's our cue to sleep," Terry informs me.

I nod and walk back over to my own bed. The slimy guy on my left is talking to a few other boys with his back to me. I take the opportunity to take off my black leather trousers and top. I fold them up and place them on the end of my bed. Sliding under the small blanket, this is the most relaxed I've felt since I arrived here. But the cool air just reminds me of how truly alone I feel in this world. A shiver slithers up my spine and I wrap my arms around myself.

"Aw, did I miss the show, girly?" the guy on my left says, laughing at me. I roll my eyes and ignore him. "My bed's big enough for two, you know," he says suggestively, wiggling his eyebrows up and down. I'm about to fire an insult back, but I get interrupted.

"Get into bed and shut your mouth, Lewis!" I look up and find the guy next to me holding the last of the big crates in his strong hands. He glares at Lewis and returns to what he's doing. Lewis mumbles something under his breath as the light above us goes out. A smile approaches my lips and I lay my head down on the pillow.

I wake up gasping for breath. Sweat drips off my forehead and my hands tremble with fear from my returning nightmare. It's always the same one. Trying to calm my breathing down, I look around the room. It must only be about three in the morning. Glancing around, I find a watch on the floor by Lewis's metal bedpost. I quickly grab it and look at the time. Three thirty. *Ugh.*

Placing the watch back down, I notice that everyone is sound asleep except for me. The bed next to mine is empty, but the boy's clothes are still sitting on the end. He must be out there, rescuing new survivors. *That's where I need to be.*

I grab a towel from under my bed and carefully make my way to the shower room. Trying not to make too much noise, I creep up the dorm and into the large space. Taking off the remainder of my clothes and running my hands through the tangles of greasy hair, I turn on the showerhead. I indulge in the warm water falling from above me, scrubbing myself raw with a bar of soap left on a shelf. However hard I scrub, I can't seem to shake the terrible flashes of my memories away. Lathering up the soap in my hand, I wash my hair until my arms start to ache.

Once I feel clean enough, I put the little white vest on with some pyjama shorts. I comb my hair through with a brush left on the side and look at my reflection in the cracked glass above the sink. The girl staring back at me isn't the girl I remember — she's a stranger. Wet blonde hair cascades down past her shoulders and her piercing green eyes peer straight through me. Dark circles underneath them remind her of the horrors she's seen. Small cuts and scrapes outline her cheekbones, the pale freckles now as dark as the circles under her eyes.

I throw my stuff back underneath my bed and slide under the small blanket once again. My heart beats ferociously in my chest. The wall I've built around it keeps me from breaking down. I close my eyes and drift off into another world of horrors.

I wake up to the sound of a horn coming from the speaker. Lewis throws a ratty old pillow over his head to block out the noise.

"DEFENCE STARTS IN TEN MINUTES! EVERYONE DOWN TO THE TRAINING ROOMS!" A male voice echoes through the dorm and then the speakers go silent. A ringing buzzes through my ears. As I look around, boys are getting out of their beds and putting on their leather training clothes. I climb out of my own bed and reach underneath, dragging out my clothes from yesterday.

"Nice legs, girly," Lewis smirks.

Quickly I get changed and pull my hair back into a ponytail. I feel eyes watching me. *I really wish they would all get on with their own business.*

"I could get used to this," Lewis says, smiling. He begins to walks off. "You coming?" He shouts at me from halfway down the dorm room. I may as well follow him since I don't know where I'm going. I hurriedly pull on my black boots and follow him out the door. We walk alongside each other until we come to a few large grey domes in front of us.

"These are the training rooms. I will enter through this one. And you will enter through that one." He points to the grey dome on the far left.

"Why?"

"Because you're new," he replies. Rolling his eyes, he leaves me and walks toward the other dome. It rises as he walks through. *Automatic doors?*

I walk over to the dome on the left and find it opens up as I step through. My eyes widen at the sight. The room is filled with training equipment. Targets with bloodred circles drawn onto them stand in the middle of the room and large menacing swords stand at the side. Enormous punching bags are attached to the ceiling. A big arena stands proudly in the middle, and metal bars run along the outside. As people start to crowd around, I wonder what they are used for.

"Let's begin. New survivors over here!" a familiar voice shouts, his gruff tone echoing through the room. I look around and find the boy whose bed is next to mine gesturing for people to gather around. He is wearing all black leather like the rest of us, but his body is strong, muscular, and toned. His dark brown hair is tousled as if he's been awake most of the night and I can make out a small square symbol on his arm. *A tattoo perhaps*? Everyone starts to walk over to him.

"My name is Troy." His voice is deep but has a soft tone to it. "You will proceed to come down here every morning to train. The more of you that show true survival skills, the more lives we can save." He walks us over to the punching bags hanging from the wall. I look around at the others, seeing their faces filled with fear and confusion. "We need as many of you to focus and train hard. In a matter of weeks you will be able to defend yourselves out there, but for now we will stick to the basics." He leans against one of the bags hanging from the ceiling with a hard expression.

A few more groups are dotted around the large training area. As they disperse around the room, each of them has a different skill. A few boys and girls grab the swords and begin to fight one another. A few others walk into the ring in the middle. I don't think

I've ever felt so out of place.

"You." A finger points at me. "What's your name?" Troy narrows his eyes at me.

"Ella." A few boys snort with laughter, but Troy glares at them until they stop.

"Well Ella, have you ever punched anything before?" He waits for my answer. All eyes are on me as I shake my head slowly. A few mumbles come from behind me, followed by laughter. "Throw a punch to this one." He gestures to the bag he's leaning on. *He can't be serious, can he?* "It's not a question." He narrows his eyes. I walk over to the punching bag and he holds it at arm's length, steadying it for me.

"Can't wait to see this." A few boys laugh at me from across the room. The other groups have stopped what they are doing and all eyes are on me. *Great.*

CHAPTER 3

I CAUTIOUSLY WALK OVER TO the punching bag and take a deep breath. I can feel the whole room watching me, their eyes burning into the back of my head. I can do this. I hold out my shaking hands in front of me and clench them into fists. Taking a deep breath, I put all of my strength into punching the bag. It doesn't even budge. That's it. They are never going to let me out there to save others. I've completely ruined it by one punch.

The whole room is filled with laughter as the groups all go about showing off their skills once again. I look around at my own group and a few of the younger girls smile at me sympathetically. Troy has no expression on his face. It's a complete blank. *Is he disappointed?*

"This is why we need to train." His voice echoes through the room and everyone quiets down. He looks at me sternly, which I can only assume means that we are done here and to stand by the others once again. I sigh as I walk back over and a few boys around me snigger amongst themselves.

"You will practice what you need to survive. Split up and train." Troy then walks off, leaving the group a little stunned and confused. Everyone disperses and crowds around the big ring in the middle. I'm intrigued as to what's happening over there, so I head over.

Pushing my way through a few taller people, I find two muscular guys fighting. They both hold the tip of their gleaming, silver swords out at each other. The first one has deep bloodied cuts on his forearm and strong muscular legs, but he doesn't give up. His eyes are filled with determination as he charges towards the other. Fire burning in his eyes, he knocks the other guy to the floor and holds him in place.

A whole room of applause breaks out as the guy holds up his weapon and walks out of the ring triumphantly. As he turns to leave he takes one more look around the crowd, his flaming eyes finding mine. My heart immediately speeds up as he looks at my weak body. Slowly, his lips curve into a smirk. I quickly look away and accidentally bump into George, nearly knocking us both to the floor.

"Whoa, slow down," he laughs. Then he looks toward the boy in the ring. "That's Jason. He's the sword-fighting champion. No one has ever come close to beating him, except Troy." George leans against the ring. I smile at him.

"Troy?" I ask.

"Yeah, he's a brilliant fighter. One of the best here. That's probably why he's training us." George shrugs. "Anyway, better get back to it. You going to be alright on your own?" I nod my answer.

"See you around." George walks off with a cheeky grin and shows off, spinning his sword on his little finger. I can't help but giggle at him and he laughs back, disappearing into the crowd.

I spend the next half an hour on the punching bags. I get a few nasty remarks aimed at me, but I can't give up.

"You'll never get any muscles doing that." Kira stands a few feet away from me. She leans against one of the bags wearing a bored expression. I turn around and find her studying me carefully. "Come with me." She gestures for me to follow. Intrigued, I follow her cautiously. Anything to get me away from all the nasty remarks.

When we leave the training room, I follow her through the dome-shaped doors and back down the dingy tunnel.

"Where are we going?" I ask, dodging a few wires hanging from the ceiling.

"Just keep quiet and follow me," she whispers.

I keep my mouth shut, passing room after room. Screams, moans, and laughter fill the air, each sound coming from different doorways. The suspense is making me uneasy and I find it hard to walk on the rocky ground as the tunnel narrows. Finally Kira stops at a grey door to her left. Pulling a keycard out from inside of her top, she types in a number on the keypad in front of her.

Looking around, I follow her into the little room filled with a variety of swords. Tall sparkling blades sit on one stand. Small, yet deadly, daggers are placed on the wall at the opposite side.

"This is where the soldiers train. I mean, look at you. You need some help, and I'm going to train you!" She smiles mischievously.

"Why?" I ask, confused.

"Why not? We need as many trained soldiers as possible, and you look like you care about those other survivors out there. Do you want the help or not?" She raises an eyebrow.

"Of course," I say, staring at the sparkling weapons filling each metal wall.

"Great, then let's start!" She grins.

CHAPTER 4

AFTER A FEW HOURS I have learnt how to use basic combat with my fists. Kira taught me to only fight when necessary.

"You don't want to get too close to what's out there." I repeat her words in my head.

"If your blood gets infected with the virus, then you'll have a matter of hours before you change into those disgusting creatures. Once you're bitten, you're gone."

She taught me never to strike first.

"The virus kills the creatures themselves over time. When you come across a weaker one, it won't be as big of a threat." Her words are etched into my mind as I repeat them over and over.

"Guns only slow them down. The only way to stop them with a bullet is a clear shot to the heart. If you want to disable them for good, a sword is your best bet. The more limbs you cut off, the harder it is for the virus to spread," she'd warned.

She taught me how to use a small blade to defend against the stronger ones. *"The younger creatures are the ones you want to look out for. They're the deadliest of them all. Increased strength, almighty aggression, and a bloodthirsty hunger that can help them rip you apart in seconds. They also have increased speed which makes it almost impossible to outrun them."*

She also taught me that even though they have increased human abilities, they have smaller brains, incapable of working together and trapping their victims.

"The most important thing to remember is not to put yourself at risk. We can't afford to lose any more survivors than we already have."

My head is throbbing from all the training as I make my way back through the dark tunnel. The dreary walls and leaking water drips from the ceiling. I squeeze through the narrow space to find more dark metal walls. Steel metal. The only thing that protects us from the virus.

This camp was built underground for our protection. They built it weeks before anyone knew what was happening. For most people it was too late. Severe numbers of attacks started. My whole town screaming. That's what I remember. My mind wanders back to the memories that haunt me every waking minute.

Running towards the front door of my house, my family and I peer outside into the street. Fires and hell has broken loose down the other side of the neighbourhood. My mum rushes back inside and smashes a hole in the wall using a brick she found from outside.

"Mum, what are you *doing*?!" my little sister Leila shrieks.

Mum's long, dark hair falls down her back in soft waves and

her long winter jacket is wrapped around her shoulders tightly. She looks at each of us with her beautiful blue eyes. Reaching inside the hardboard wall, Mum grabs two big bags from inside, handing one to my dad. My dad looks up and knowingly grabs it. His short, brown tousled hair stands up on end. He wears his long black coat and gazes at our family with those emerald green eyes. He then huddles us in a little group.

"What the hell is going on?!" my older brother Henry asks, panicking.

"Listen kids, we don't have much time. Once we get outside, I want you to run as quickly as you can to the edge of town. A truck should be waiting there. Get in it and away from here. It will take you to safety." Dad holds us all close. Henry looks around in horror as if the stormy snow clouds are crashing to earth.

"If the possibility that some of us don't make it-"

"What?!" I ask, terrified.

"Carry on running. Don't stop until you get there. Promise me!" Dad looks at us all sternly. The three of us all look at each other with confused and horrified expressions. "If any of you get bitten, just stop running. You'll be a danger to everyone else." Dad looks at the floor with tears watering the deep green.

"You must leave each other behind if one of you gets bitten, but me and your father will help as much as we can." Mum pleads with us. "No matter how hard it is, just keep running to the truck. Do you understand me?"

"Yes," we all say together. I look round at the others, tears trickle down Leila's pale cheeks. Henry wraps an arm around my shoulder. He looks at me as if it's the last time he will ever see me. We all hear a scream from outside getting closer and closer.

"What's going on?!" Henry still demands, running towards the door.

"Ready?" Mum walks over to Henry and puts a soft hand on

his shoulder, holding back her own tears.

"Ready," I say. Mum gives each of us all a small, silver knife from inside the brown bag. Leila looks up at Mum quizzically.

"You'll need it," is all she says as she steps out of the front door. I look around at the red roses outlining the frame. This may be the last time I ever see my home. I take a deep breath and eventually turn away from the house I grew up in. We all follow behind as we begin to run. Henry is faster so he races ahead.

"Keep running!" Mum shouts.

I hold Leila's hand as we run together. Screaming and shouting surrounds us. I hear a high-pitched scream behind me and turn my head around. A creature so horrifying with diseased, grey skin hanging from its face growls into the atmosphere. A disturbing smell of raw flesh oozes through the air. Mum holds the knife up to the creature, trying to get away. Its sharp teeth tear through her arm and red blood seeps out from the injury. The gore runs down her lifeless body. Mum's lips part as a small cry for help escapes her lungs, but the sound is weak and fragile as her body turns white and still.

"MUM!" I shout, turning to run toward her. I need to help her. Save her.

"No!" Dad runs at me and pushes me away. "Keep on going!" he shouts over the chaos. I can't do it. I can't leave Mum!

"You need to leave her, Ella. Please…" Dad's eyes water.

In that one second, I play back every memory, every song she's ever sung me, every word she's ever said. Those soft lips that kiss me goodnight. The sweet honest heart that has now stopped beating. Everything in my world has crumbled down. I have nothing left to live for. Not Mum. *Please*. No.

I have to help her. I need to help her. I immediately grasp my fingers around the silver blade in my hand and aim straight for the monster looming over her. The knife glides through the air and pierces the creature straight through the heart. After watching the monster's body land on the gravel, I run over to where Mum lays in the middle of the road. Cars have stopped and people are fleeing from the horrific scene. I crumble to my knees as I hold her head in my shaking hands.

"Mum." I try to wake her. "No, Mum. *Please* wake up. Please." I hold onto her hair, the brown strands loosely dangling to the ground. Her fluorescent blue eyes are now closed and dull of life. "Mum, *please* wake up." My eyes shut in pain. Tears roll down my ice-cold cheeks and my lips tremble in agony. I've never thought of the last words I'd say to someone. Nor did I ever think I'd have to say them. Those three words — the strongest and most powerful words that could leave my lips. "I love you, Mum." I bring her close to me and lay her head down on the curb. My whole world has shattered.

Dad finally approaches and pulls me away from her body. I can't hear what he's saying. Each sound and every single heartbeat are drowned out. Eventually I shake away the tears as I fight against every ounce of strength I have to keep on running. I need to protect Leila.

I grab Leila's small hand and we run alongside Dad, hearing more shouts and horrific shrieks from inside passing houses. A couple of deadly creatures line up in front of us a few meters away, blocking our path. They corner a few of our neighbours into small alleyways down the side of our street. I know they're not going to survive, so I grab Leila's hand even tighter as she runs beside me. I look down and find her little face is swollen from crying. Her skinny legs sprint as fast as they can. Dad eventually picks her up in his arms and we speed up to outrun the rest of the monsters.

"Nearly there!" he shouts, breathlessly.

Suddenly a creature runs for us. My eyes widen, standing between Dad and the monster. It continues to run at full speed, hungry eyes and jagged claws waiting to rip us apart. As it gets closer, I can smell the lingering disease drooling from its skin. Dad freezes, my sister in his arms. I stand in front of them, holding out my knife. I get ready to fight as it lunges for us.

"Ella! NO!" Dad shouts, placing Leila on the ground. But from nowhere, Henry jumps on the monster's back and hurls it out of the way.

"NO! Henry!" I scream, as the creature takes a ferocious bite into Henry's leg. His face is pure torture as red liquid bubbles to the top of his wound. His skin turns pale white as I look away. I turn around to see my dad's horrified expression. I fight back the anger, tears welling up inside of me. We must carry on. We must get to safety. Henry has sacrificed himself for us. I have to stay strong.

"Come on!" I shout, reaching down to grab Leila's hand, but it's not there. I spin around, looking for her.

"Leila? LEILA!" I run backwards and suddenly find my dad's body lying on the ground, turning paler by the second. My mouth gapes open. I can't move. Everyone I love is dying.

"Ella?" a little voice behind me murmurs. I turn around quickly to find a shaking Leila, holding her arm. I crumble to my knees in front of her.

"No, Leila." I put my head to hers as the hot, burning tears cascade down my face. Not Leila. No. Her hand covers her bite, concealing the blood and raw flesh.

"Run, Ella." Leila's little face looks up at me, her deep brown eyes filled with terror.

"Run, Ella. You can make it." Her skin starts to turn pale. I hold her head in my hands.

"No, I can't leave you. I can't..."

"Go, Ella. Please." Tears stream down her face while she pleads with me. I clench my eyes shut from the pain and agony that's ripping through my heart. I can't do it! I can't leave her too.

"Ella, go!" Her eyes become distant and start to turn grey as her skin turns white and diseased.

"No!" I cry, my hands now shaking uncontrollably. Her expression turns blank and she looks up at me with empty grey eyes. Her body starts to sway, before falling lifelessly to the floor. I grab the knife from her little hand and stand up. I look up through my watering eyes with venom filling my soul. I wipe away each tear with my sleeve and run.

Creatures lunge for me, but I fight back. Using the knife, I stab them out of my way, finally seeing a clear light up ahead. A few others run alongside me, fighting off the last of the monsters as we all come face to face with a large black truck. Strong muscular soldiers stand helping us onto the back. We all sit down as the vehicle drives off.

The whole of Redcross. Population four thousand. Only four survivors.

"Ella! There you are!" I snap out of my memories and wipe away a tear lingering on my cheek.

Looking up, I find Terry, George, and Jim walking towards me. Jim's dark hair falls into his eyes as he regards me with a concerned expression.

"Ella, is everything alright?" Jim asks. He waits for my reaction.

"Yes, I'm fine. Just thinking," I reply. George and Terry look at me sympathetically. They're probably wondering how a girl like me could ever survive a virus attack.

"Come on, let's get some food inside of you. You'll waste away," George teases, nudging me and smiling.

The Rep hall is filled with tables and chairs, contrasting against the deep red walls. The lights shine down, hanging above us all. People fill the room, all sitting around eating and chatting. Jim leads me towards a table in the middle of the crowded room and I sit down. George and Terry soon join us. The atmosphere is filled with boys laughing and girls fluttering their eyelids at them. I roll my eyes, blankly staring at the food in front of me. How can they be laughing and chatting at a time like this?

A large bowl of pasta and some kind of red sauce sits in the middle, plates of dry bread surrounding it. Picking up a spoon, I take some pasta out of the huge bowl and place it onto the chipped plate in front of me. To be honest, I don't feel very hungry. All I want to do is save those poor, starving survivors out there. People are happily eating away in here, but what about the others? Do they have any food out there? Are people starving? I push the plate away, feeling too guilty to eat it.

"The food not up to your standards?" A small smile layers on Jim's face and he raises an eyebrow.

"No, it's not that," I reply.

"You need to build up your strength, Ella. You want to become stronger, right?" George looks at me. *Finally*, someone talking sense.

"Eat it. You'll feel better." He smiles and I smile back. A little dimple lights up on his cheek which makes me think back to my brother. *Henry*. I think about his sacrifice. His love for us. He died for us. I push the plate further away and rise from the table.

"Ella, what's wrong?" Terry's eyes widen in concern. I can't look at him without breaking down in tears, so I silently walk away from the table. I'm not going to sit around happily eating while there are other survivors out there. I need to train. I need to become stronger.

"Where you going, girly?" I bump straight into a tall figure in front of me. "If you wanted to touch me, all you had to do was ask." A sly grin creeps up Lewis's face. *Ugh.* I walk around him but he blocks my path. Rolling my eyes, I look up at him. Are we really going to play this game?

"I said, where'd you think you're going?" His grin only widens.

"None of your business." I shove past him. He moves over to let me by as a few catcalls come from behind me. I don't look back. I run down the dark tunnel, back to the boy's dorm, thankful that it's empty for once. When I reach my bed, I begin to rummage around in my clothes, locating a new pair of leather trousers and top buried underneath everything else. I take off my clothes and fold them up on the end of my bed.

Footsteps sound from the end of the dormitory and when I look up I spot Troy walking over with his own leather training clothes on. The black top clings to every one of his rippling muscles and he is wearing some black boots that squelch with every step. As his eyes find mine, I notice the deep hazel and I can't help but melt a little inside.

The strong contours of his face and the tanned skin is any girl's dream. I bet he has them all bowing at his feet. Why am I even thinking about this? What would he ever want with me? I shake the thought away, noticing his expression stays blank. I quickly tear my eyes away from him and pull on my new clean clothes. Carefully watching me, he sits on the edge of his bed.

"Why aren't you in the Rep hall?" he asks.

I look up, surprised. "What do you mean?"

"Why aren't you in the Rep hall?" he repeats simply. His lips twitch into the smallest of smiles and his face looks slightly amused. My cheeks start to blush under his watchful gaze.

"I wasn't hungry." I pull on a pair of black fingerless gloves.

"Come with me." He gets up and gestures for me to follow him. I narrow my eyes. Where is he taking me?

"Do you want to survive?" He raises an eyebrow at me before disappearing into the hallway. I quickly grab my boots, sliding them on, and scramble to catch up with him.

I follow him until we get to the same room Kira took me to the day before. He takes out a keycard from deep inside his pocket and places the plastic into the glowing blue slot on the keypad. The light glows green as the door automatically opens before us. He types in a code and walks through the doorway. I am close on his heels when he suddenly grabs a sword from the wall and throws it at me in a quick flash. *Whoa!* I catch it by the handle, surprising myself.

"Your reflexes are good." He looks at me from over his shoulder. I walk towards him, holding the sword by the handle. *Gosh,* it weighs a ton. As I look around, I familiarise myself with the training room. Brown punching bags hang down and different sized swords scatter along each metal wall.

"Straight to the heart. That's the best way to kill them." Troy looks at me, his gaze never leaving mine. I look at the sword in my hand. The blade shines and the tip glistens. The handle, made out of thick red metal fits my hand perfectly. Curling my fingers around it, I feel a rush of warmth, a slight beacon of hope that whirls through my veins.

"If those creatures are coming at you from behind, what should you do?" He waits patiently for my answer. What *would* I do? I have no idea.

"Swing around and stab them, I guess." I shrug, not knowing what else to say.

"There is no guessing. Once you're out there, you must know their every move, their every thought before they know it themselves." His eyes turn dark and stern as he walks over holding out a punching bag in front of me. *Not again.*

"You would have to turn to physical contact if you lose your weapon." He studies me. Walking over, I look at the bag and then at Troy.

"Go on. If you were being attacked, how would you respond..." I whack the bag as hard as I can, dropping the sword to the floor. The metal vibrates against the ground and the sound causes me to shiver. He doesn't flinch. I whack it again using my fists. Again and again, but he doesn't look impressed.

"Use your whole body, not just your fists," he encourages. I take a deep breath and picture a creature, skin hanging from its face, teeth as sharp as knives. Bones piercing through its gruesome flesh. It attacks Leila and I run at it. I feel the anger and pain coursing through my bones as the creature digs its teeth into Leila.

"NOOO!" Shouting, I punch the bag so hard that Troy stumbles back a little.

"Good, keep going." Looking surprised, he holds it back in place.

Using my fists, I punch. Using my elbows, I knock it from side to side. I dodge the bag when it comes straight towards me and punch it again. I think of Leila and the horrible monster driving its teeth into her poor little arm. I smack the bag harder as it flies toward Troy. I get an image of my brother tackling the disgusting creature to the ground. He jumps on its back and I just stand there, looking at the horror before me. The image distracts me long enough for the bag to fly back towards me, knocking me in my side and causing me to fall to the floor. My elbows hit the ground and I wince in pain. No pain can compare to the emptiness I feel inside, the loss of everyone I love.

"You okay?" Troy helps me up.

"I'm fine." I dust off the dirt and look up. His face is inches from mine and my body instantly heats up. His expression searches mine. My heartbeat thumps wildly. I can hear the rapid beat of his own heart deep inside his chest. He quickly looks away, frowning, and steadies the bag hanging from the ceiling.

"That was good." He puts everything back into place. Sauntering back over, he stops next to my side. "Fight with your heart. Do not get distracted," he says, and then leaves the room. My heart is left beating rapidly and my side hurting. I run back out of the doorway, hearing it close behind me.

CHAPTER 5

FIGHT WITH MY HEART.

I keep replaying the sentence over and over again. Digging up the hurt and anger over losing my family. Letting the pure pain rip through me every time I fight. The agony of losing so many loved ones. I can't take it — the memories are too much. Once I begin to think about it, I shut everyone else out. I have buried my feelings so deep my soul feels numb. I need to be out there, saving people, rescuing lives, the way the soldiers should have done for my family. I didn't even get a chance to say goodbye.

Walking back through the dingy tunnel, I finally find the doorway back into the dormitories. The lights flicker above me from the lack of power and the damp water drips down from the ceiling, creating small ripples in the puddles surrounding my feet. Just as I thought, the room is filled with boys again. I guess they've all finished eating.

"We were getting worried, girly," a guy's voice comes from my left, as I walk down toward my bed.

"Not running out on us, are we?" Another shoves past me and laughs with his friends. They all look me up and down. I take a deep breath and ignore them all.

Sitting on the edge of my bed, I look over to Jim, Terry, and George. They are all huddled in a little group talking. Troy's bed is empty yet again. He must use the evenings to go out there. Bringing home new survivors.

A few whistles come from my right and some vulgar comments echo from down the hall.

"Alright darling, wanna share my bed?" A guy whistles.

"Come to join us, babe?" Another one laughs and calls out.

"Hush down, boys." A familiar female voice comes from the doorway. I look around and find Kira walking down the dorm room towards me. She walks with confidence, rolling her eyes at the whistles from a few guys behind her. They look her up and down with their tongues hanging out, like she's a Greek goddess.

"Two girls? This calls for a little party." Lewis raises his eyebrows at me. His slimy grin returns. He really needs to learn some boundaries.

Kira raises her eyebrows up with an annoyed expression and suddenly lunges for Lewis. She quickly clasps a sword out of her belt and grabs him by the collar. Taking him by surprise, she holds him against the wall. The tip of her blade rests against his throat while she smiles innocently. Lewis's eyes are wide in shock as the other boys around the room stop and stare.

"Shut your mouth, Lewis!" Kira smirks at him, letting go. Lewis is left standing there, confused. The other boys around the room burst out laughing.

"Hey, Ella." Kira stands in front of me, helping me off the bed.

"Hey." I return her smile.

All eyes are on us. Well, probably more on Kira. Her brown

hair cascades down past her shoulders, and her leather clothes cling around her perfect curves. I envy her perfect looks a little. She looks at me with those sparkling green eyes and has a mischievous look creeping up her face.

"I have a job for you." Her smile widens.

"What's that?" I ask, intrigued.

Her cheeks light up and she whispers, "It's a secret. Come with me." She grabs my arm and pulls me out of the dorm room. Some more disgusting comments get thrown our way, but I choose to block them out.

"Want me to join you?" A voice drifts off into the distance as the door closes behind me. Kira drags me through the dark tunnel, our own footsteps echoing behind us. The damp water continues to drip from the ceiling while we make our way down the tunnel. We start to hear the thunder of more footsteps coming our way.

"Who's tha…?" I start, but she covers my mouth with her hand and drags me into the nearest room. We stand there in the dark, hiding from the marching footsteps that are getting closer. My heart starts to beat furiously. With every breath, the footsteps get louder, thudding against the ground. Kira's eyes have widened at the sound, coming closer and closer. Her stern expression tells me to keep quiet, so I listen to the silent beat of my heart. Kira's hand is clasped over my mouth so tightly it's hard to breathe.

Soon we start to hear voices. Two male voices. Kira spins us around so we stand just inside the door, out of sight.

"Derrick wants us to pick up new survivors?" one says.

"Ha, like he'd ever go out there himself," says the other, a deeper voice than the first.

"Come on. He only wants more bloody survivors to cooperate with his system. He is greedy for power and we all know it!"

"I don't know why we have to do his dirty work though."

"Isn't it obvious? He wants to create an army. An army strong enough to take down The Society." The deep voice laughs.

"Like he'd ever be able to do that," the other one chuckles.

Soon enough they both walk off, back down the tunnel. Kira takes her hand away from my mouth. Finally I can breathe again. The Society? What is that?

"Stay quiet and follow me," she whispers.

I continue to follow Kira down the dark tunnel once again. Our footsteps are loud and I hope it doesn't attract too much attention. After a few minutes we come to a halt. Kira stops in the middle of the hallway, raising her hand to the air before turning back towards me.

"This whole place is full of cameras," she whispers, looking around warily. "You ready?"

Ready for what? The lights suddenly go out and the hallway is now pitch-black. What the...?

A breath gets caught in my throat as I panic, trying to squint my eyes in the darkness. What's going on?! A hand grabs my arm and I fight it off.

"Hey, it's me," Kira's stern voice whispers. "Come on!" She grabs me by the arm again and pulls me through the dark. We take a few sharp turns left and I bump into a few steel walls while we run through the darkness. I can't see ahead of me at all, so I hope Kira knows where she's going.

A small breeze whisks past through my hair as we continue to sprint through each corridor. A dirty, musty smell lingers in the air surrounding us. Finally the lights come back on and we stop running. Kira lets go of my arm and stands in front of me with her hands on her knees, catching her breath.

"Right. Ella, we are going to save some lives. You ready?" She flings a sword at me and smiles. I catch it effortlessly, which surprises me yet again.

"We are what?" I look up confused and out of breath.

"I'm taking you out there. You want to help, right?" She raises an eyebrow. I don't have time to answer since she walks off towards a few glass doors.

The clear glass is stained with a huge yellow symbol. I have only a few seconds to study it before they open up in front of us. Kira walks through and stands on a circular platform. The floor is made of iron with mouldy, grey pipes and cables running along the walls. Each one sparks occasionally and a little keypad stands in the doorway. When I step through into the small compact room, the doors close behind me, and the air slowly gets sucked out of my lungs.

"B-but I'm not ready," I say, stuttering.

"Of course you are. You only need to know how to defend yourself. You're not going to be one of Derrick's army." She rolls her eyes and the floor starts to lift up like an elevator. *One of Derrick's army?*

I steady myself by grabbing onto one of the pipes on the wall. The ground pushes us upwards, until I start to breathe in the fresh crisp air.

The outside world stands before us. The cool breeze whisks past my cheeks, flowing through my blonde hair. A clear and frosty smell runs straight through my veins, causing me to shiver. The deserted, empty land spreads out for miles and a tall metal gate surrounds us, protecting the camp from what's out there. It stands proud, shadowing us. The sun is starting to set, glowing close to the rubble covering the dusty ground. Kira locks the metal lift on the floor using a little golden key and gestures for me to follow.

She picks up her speed and runs toward a big pickup truck, standing by the Iron Gate doors. A couple of soldiers lean against it. *Surely they won't allow me to come with them, will they?* The soldiers both wear metal shoulder pads and leather body armour. They both have short haircuts and carry a variety of weapons in their belts.

"You coming?" Kira shouts, from the front. I jog over towards them as Kira high fives the taller one.

"Mark! Long time, no see!" she laughs. He smiles, a cheeky grin on his face. His piercing blue eyes gaze at Kira when she high fives him. Mark has got very broad shoulders and his black top clings to every muscle.

The other soldier is leaning against the wheel of the truck. He seems somewhat more reserved than Mark. His dark hair hides his eyes while he watches me. Kira nods at him.

"Dale," she says, bluntly. He returns her nod and climbs into the driver's seat of the truck.

"Who's the newbie?" Mark rakes his eyes over me, narrowing them slightly. He is covered from head to toe in weapons and tattoos. Swords, guns, bullets…you name it. He doesn't look much older than me and Kira, but his blue eyes hold a certain fascination.

"This is Ella," Kira smiles. "She's cool." She climbs into the truck with Mark, who is giving her a helping hand. His hand conveniently slips from her waist, moving downwards, but she quickly slaps his hand away. He just laughs.

"Hands to yourself!" She shoves him away using her strong legs. He stumbles backward and I giggle. Mark turns toward me.

"You need a leg up?" His cheeky grin widens.

"No, I've got it, thanks." I take a deep breath and run, jumping onto the seat in the back. He looks at me momentarily shocked and impressed, but shakes it off.

"Let's go!" Mark shouts. Dale starts up the truck and it speeds off.

The wind whisks past us. I enjoy the fresh air and the new scenery. Even though the ground is just dirt with a few new buds of grass growing, it's still better than metal walls. The sky is turning darker and I can start to see the glistening moon appearing above the mountains. The boys start to playfully howl like wolves, their voices echoing through the air as Kira joins in. Smiling, I look back out of the window. The glass has been taken out, so it's just a hole in the truck door really.

After a few miles we pass by a few bushes every so often. The sky is pitch-black now, with the moonlight shining down on a few sparkling lakes that run through every hill and curve of the earth. Dale switches on the headlights and carries on driving. I twist my sword around in my hand and the tip glistens in the moonlight. The handle is inscribed with the letter 'E.' *Is that for Ella?* I look up to find Kira's eyes watching me.

"We each have our own sword." She holds up hers with the letter 'K' etched into the handle.

"Thank you," I say, smiling.

"It's no big deal, you're part of the crew now." Her grin widens.

"Yeah, but you'll have to do the secret pact first." Mark smiles mischievously.

"What's that?" I look up at him with wary eyes.

He wiggles both of his eyebrows in suggestion. *I think I know what that means.* Kira shoves him hard in the side and he laughs.

"Only messing."

"She's off the menu anyway." Kira grins. Mark frowns and looks at me.

"You are?" He raises an eyebrow and Dale looks at me in the

rearview mirror.

Before I can say another word, Kira jumps in. "Come on, I see the way Troy looks at you, Ella. He's never looked at any girl like that before." She nudges me in the arm.

"What do you mean?" I reply, not knowing what else to say.

"I mean, he can't keep those simply *gorgeous* brown eyes off of you. Every girl wants him…he's like a Greek god but he's always kept to himself." She smiles.

"Even a few guys want him." Mark nudges me, winking. I laugh and roll my eyes. A few buildings start to come into view in front of us. The doors and windows have been smashed and the place is deserted. No sign of any living souls. The air starts to smell funny — like a weird stuffy locker room.

"Shhh." Dale raises his hand and the truck slows down. We all cautiously look around outside, but can't see anything. The smell becomes stronger, twirling around us. The cool night air sends a chill up my spine as we all grow wary. The faint smell of rotting enters the air and I hold my hand over my nose to block it out. A sudden growl comes from behind us. We all turn around to see the most horrifying creature standing on the back of the truck. Its teeth gleam in the moonlight as it cries out in a deathly howl.

CHAPTER 6

BLACKENED, DISEASED SKIN HANGS FROM its face. The pale, white spots pierce the rotting skin on its deadly arms. Jagged bones hang off the raw flesh, slowly decaying off of the creature. The stench that oozes from the horrific monster lingers in the air. The truck doesn't stop, but speeds up instead. Dale slams his foot on the gas pedal, and the truck hurls forward. Kira and Mark both have their swords out, ready to fight. The fire burning in their eyes show the hatred they have towards these creatures. When the truck gains speed, the creature stumbles backward, falling onto its side. It barely moves.

"It's not a young one, Ella. They're the ones you need to watch out for. This one hasn't got much longer left," Kira says, placing a hand on my shoulder.

"How long has it got?" I ask.

Kira puts away her sword as the creature tumbles off the back of the truck. It lays in the middle of the dirt road behind us. Its body lays mangled, disappearing into the distance when the truck travels on at a quick speed.

"I would say a couple of hours, Ella. They carry a disease around with them. Eventually the virus kills the creature itself over time," she replies. Kira then puts her sword down by her legs and ties it to her belt, letting it hang down past her waist.

"Zombies." Mark winks at me.

"Zombies? I thought they were extinct?" I ask.

"We all thought they were extinct, but the virus is spreading everywhere. They are back, Ella. It's our job to help survivors out there. We've got to save the world," Kira smirks. *I guess.*

"Zombies are vile, disgusting creatures and the more that die, the better," Dale adds. His voice is deep, but soft. He slows the truck down gradually.

"Right, Ella. We are going to scope out this town. We've found a few survivors here before, and there might be more. Stay aware of your surroundings and don't get bitten." Kira smirks. She jumps out of the moving vehicle, grasping her hand around the handle of her gleaming sword. Ready to defend herself, she lands flawlessly on the ground as the dust swirls up from the floor. I watch her gracious landing with complete awe.

"Come on, Ella. Jump out!" Mark gets ready to jump and urges me to follow. I slowly grasp the outside of the truck and pull myself through the window. I climb onto the roof and find my feet. I take one last look at the ground before closing my eyes. In one swift movement, I jump and the adrenaline rushes through my veins at the sudden free fall. I hit the dirt floor beneath me. The dust on the ground swirls around my feet and an electric current pulses up through my legs. I turn around to find Mark grinning at me.

"What?" I ask, brushing off the dirt from my trousers.

"Nothing, you're just different from what I expected." He smiles and runs toward Kira. I follow behind, attaching my sword to my belt. It hangs down in its leather case, and somehow I feel comforted by the fact that I have a way to protect myself. Dale then drives off with the truck, the squeak of tires quite audible.

"Where's Dale going?" I watch him drive off behind us.

"He's circling the perimeter. If anything's wrong, he'll honk the horn," Kira replies.

A small town of houses stand in front of us, a thick layer of dust and dirt surrounding it. The cottages may have once been a beautiful place to live — bright green gardens and roses blooming in the sun, with white doors gleaming and windows sparkling. Now stands a stranded town, doors smothered in blood and the glass in the windows dangerous with pointed edges. A gloomy silence fills the atmosphere as we all look around carefully.

"Check each house for supplies, survivors, and perhaps any new weapons you can find. Ella and I will go together," Kira says, taking charge. Mark nods his assent at her.

"Whoever finds the most wins!" he shouts, running off into a house on our left. Kira laughs and shakes her head. We walk on the dusty road in the middle of the street.

"This place is too quiet." Kira narrows her eyes and I hold my hand over the handle of my sword, just in case.

"Come on, let's check over there." She leads me into a house on our right and pushes the bloodied front door open carefully. The wooden floor creaks, interrupting the spine chilling silence.

"Anyone in here?" Kira shouts through the doorway. After a few seconds, we get no reply. "I'll take that as a no." She walks through the doorway as a rotten smell of death fills my senses.

"You take upstairs and I'll check down here." She walks off through another doorway and disappears.

I step over dead decaying bodies on the ground while I search the house. Hanging pictures on the walls are torn and wonky. The dull, orange wallpaper hangs from the damp plaster. A few rats run across the floor leaving little footprints behind them. They disappear into a small hole at the bottom of the house. Blood is splattered over every inch of furniture. I take a deep steeling breath and walk over the raised floorboards, making my way up the stairs. Each one creaks with every small step. As I get closer to the landing, the air becomes stuffier. "Anyone in here?" I shout.

No answer.

Cautiously, I tread down the upstairs hallway. I look into a room on my left and find a child's bedroom. It's filled with photographs and toys covering every inch of the room. A little doll sits on the bed. I walk over and pick up the ragged old toy in my hand. It reminds me of Leila — we used to collect these when we were younger. Its black buttoned eyes sparkle and the red fabric dress has a few spots of green blood staining it. Pushing back the tears, I place the doll back down. Innocent children are dying because of this dreadful disease. Images of poor helpless children running away from zombies fill my head. I shake them out and carry on to the next room. The air is becoming stuffier by the second so I hold my hand over my nose, blocking out the lingering smell of rotting death.

I walk through the last door, looking into the room. Two diseased zombies turn around and glare at me. The small white spots invade their burnt, blackened skin. Their distant, grey eyes take me in. Their jagged teeth are yellow with bits of flesh hanging out of the side. Drool seeps out of their mouths as they both look at each other. The smell spreads through the air and out into the hallway. They both run for me and I let out a bloodcurdling scream. All of a sudden Kira's footsteps can be heard running up the stairs. The trucks horn honks from in the distance and we can hear Mark's cry for help coming from outside.

The two revolting, deadly beings stalk towards me. For a minute I feel like fleeing and running in the opposite direction, but my feet are glued to the floor. I turn my head around to face them. The utterly repulsing creatures drip with disease. Quickly, I remind myself of what they've done to my family. I remember Leila's terrified little face, the cold empty tears that fell down her pale cheeks, and all I can see before me is murder. I don't wait for Kira. I don't wait for anyone. I grab my sword by the handle and charge them.

My hands burn with scorching flames as I slash the sword straight through the heart of the first one. My flawless, swift movements cut straight through the hanging flesh of the zombie. Its eyes widen as it lets out a deep cry of pain. I take a deep breath and look down at the rotting corpse on the floor. I hear a growl rumbling behind me and I twirl around to catch the other zombie about to dig its sharp teeth into my arm. I whip my sword straight into its chest as deep as it can go. A sudden relief of pain floats up from within the anger I keep buried and I let out a scream — not a scream of being terrified, but of being in control. Control over these monsters that are destroying the world. Another weak growl of pain enters the atmosphere when both zombies fall to the floor. I drag my sword back out of the creature's heart and wipe it off on the rotting wallpaper.

Kira suddenly runs in and stares wide-eyed at the two creatures on the floor. Her shocked expression soon turns into a massive grin and she pulls me into a hug.

"I knew I chose you for a reason!" For a minute I feel proud. That soon fades away when we hear Mark's screaming coming from outside. Another honk of a horn invades the atmosphere, slightly closer than the last. Kira and I turn around quickly and head to the end of the upstairs hallway.

"Help!" We can hear Mark calling from the street. *Oh no.*

We run down the stairs, almost falling over one another and dodge the gaping holes in the wooden floorboards. When we finally reach the chilly night air, we stand at the doorway with both our swords drawn, ready to attack. Sprinting down the porch, we look down the deserted street to find at least ten zombies stalking towards Mark. They all carry hunger within their eyes. Hunger for new virgin flesh.

"Mark!" Kira calls out, sprinting after him.

"Kira, no!" I run after her. The disgusting creatures turn towards Kira as she slashes away, chopping off heads and stabbing them straight in the chest. My senses are filled with an odour so strong it starts to make me dizzy.

I know as soon as my feet leave the porch that it will be a mistake, but I run towards the chaos anyway.

The zombies look up, suddenly aware of my presence and I gulp. Four monsters run for me so I twist around, grabbing my sword once again. I stab the one in front of me and as I drag the sword back out of its chest, green blood covers the tip of the blade. I shiver in disgust as I swing my sword around and catch one sneaking up on me from behind. I stab another one and another one. *Where are they all coming from?* Another honk of a horn comes from nearby and I look up, distracted. In that split second, a creature tackles me — the kind of rugby tackle my dad used to watch on TV.

Its skin isn't as diseased as the others so it must be a newly made zombie...a dangerous zombie. It snarls at me while I hold it off using my sword. The gleaming blade mirrors my terrified reflection — my hollow green eyes that scream for help and my trembling bottom lip that is now scarred by a slash of blood. The zombie lunges, pushing me to the floor, with me kicking and squirming underneath it, screaming for help. *I can't let it bite me, I can't!*

I push with all my strength, but it's no use. The creature bares its yellow, stained teeth and locks its target. I close my eyes, awaiting the agony about to enter my body, but nothing comes. The struggle with the creature is no more because it gets lifted off me. *What's happening?*

I look up to see Troy dressed head-to-toe in his tight leather clothes. He holds out his own sword while the nauseating zombie lay at his feet. My heart hammers inside my chest and I can't control my breathing when he comes over to me. I don't know whether it's from the zombie attack or from Troy standing over my body, but my heart doesn't slow down. Instead, it speeds up rapidly. The feeling is new to me and I can't help but gawk at my saviour. His body is covered in deep cuts and bruises and glistening sweat has formed around each one of his muscles.

"Need a hand?" He smiles and helps me off the floor. I smile gratefully back at him and brush the dirt off my trousers.

"Thank you." I look up at him.

"Don't mention it." He returns my gaze and then wipes off the end of his sword. I quickly see the 'T' engraved onto the handle as he slides it carefully back into its case.

"Where are the others?" I ask.

He looks around and walks forward. I hear another of Mark's shouts and I hear Kira screaming. If I could communicate telepathically with Troy, then we'd probably both be thinking the same thing. We quickly look at one another with alarm plastered on our faces, and then sprint in the direction of the chaos. I hold out my sword, ready to fight, as we run alongside each other. I keep up with Troy's long strides and I think this slightly amuses him, considering how short my legs are. We finally come across a gap between two buildings while the air nips at my skin. The dark alleyway before us stands damp and groggy. Large dustbins with buzzing flies wisp through the fog and out of the corner of my eye, I see Troy walking ahead into the silence. Kira and Mark can no longer be heard. The smoky air has wrapped its way around my skinny ankles, and I can't help but shiver from the spike of cold wind.

The fog seems to be getting stronger and it's getting even harder to see anything now. After finally deciding to follow Troy into the alleyway, I walk into the fog...reluctantly. One, I don't want to be left on my own in this creepy town, and two, I have this gut feeling that Troy could use some help fighting off whatever's in here. My boots hit dirty puddles underneath my feet and the tall brick buildings loom over us. Small washing lines are hung overhead with damp clothing still dangling from them. When I look closer, I notice most of the clothes are stained in red and green blood. My eyes widen as we suddenly hear another scream. Speeding up, I catch up to Troy and we run toward the noise. Troy holds his silver sword out in front of him, staying aware. As the fog clears, I can see a group of deadly zombies. They have cornered Kira and Mark against an old brick wall at the end of the alleyway. They are trapped. The creatures move at a slow pace, and once again, I block out the dreadful stench reeking from them.

I run forwards in front of Troy, ignoring his hand trying to grasp onto my arm to hold me back. I don't waste a second while I run for the group of zombies. I stab the first one in its back, catching the others off guard. *I guess our silent cover is blown.* It falls in front of me and I swipe the sword and pierce another right in the heart.

"You're quite a fighter, you know that?" Troy hides a smile as he steps in front of my body, shielding me from the rest of the monsters. He slashes his sword around and kills the last few surrounding us. Kira and Mark have joined in and soon enough all of the zombies are lying on the ground, their decomposing bodies disturbing the crisp air.

The horn of the truck honks from behind us and we all turn around to see Dale opening the Land Rover door. Taking a running jump, I follow Kira and Mark into the backseat. Troy places his hands on my waist and for a moment, I can't think of anything else except his warm skin against my own. But soon enough, he hoists me up into the vehicle, climbing in after me and closing the door.

"We kicked some real zombie ass!" Kira laughs and Mark joins in.

"You realise, you could of got Ella killed?" Troy glares at them, but then softens his expression when he notices my bleeding lip.

"But we didn't. So come on, lighten up, soldier." Kira nudges him but his expression doesn't change.

"Ella, you are the newest member of the zombie club," Mark chuckles.

"Thanks," I say, looking up at Troy. He meets my gaze and then looks away with a hard expression.

CHAPTER 7

WE TRAVEL BACK THE WAY we came, passing nothing but dirt. No houses, no towns, just a load of dust and dirt layering the ground. Sometimes a small bud of grass grows, peeking up through the rocks. The small amount of life on this planet is the only hope I live for at the moment. New life means hope. Hope means there is still a small chance of recovering from this ordeal. A chance to beat the virus and live peacefully once again.

"How did you find us?" Kira raises an eyebrow at Troy. He just looks at her. How *did* he find us?

"He was probably out searching for survivors until he heard Mark screaming," Dale laughs from the driver's seat. I hold back a giggle of my own and I think Dale notices, but Kira doesn't hold hers back as she playfully winds Mark up.

"I was not screaming," Mark mumbles, tracing the bold lines on one of his many tattoos.

"Yes, you were. Zombies are attacking me, help!" Kira mimics his voice perfectly and Dale starts to chuckle again.

"I did not say that!" Mark pushes Kira over on her seat and she rolls around giggling. I can't help but smile at the two of them, and I can see Mark hiding back a smile of his own while he watches Kira laugh, adoration filling his eyes.

"Help me, I'm afraid of zombies!" Kira laughs harder and Mark rolls his eyes.

"I could hear you screaming from a mile off." Troy leans back in the seat and looks up. Kira bursts out laughing again as Mark scowls at Troy. Somehow Troy doesn't notice as his gaze gets pulled back towards what he's holding. His strong palm is tightly clasped around the handle of his sword, twisting it from side to side. The small glistening light from the moon reflects against the metal, forming small gleaming patterns on the floor of the truck. I watch him carefully for a while, mesmerised by the patterns he's creating, but as soon as he senses me watching him I drag my eyes away. Like my mother always said: *curiosity killed the cat.*

When the truck finally reaches a stop, we all jump out. Kira brushes away the dust off the ground, revealing the circular elevator. The symbol outlining the elevator is a bold letter 'L' and it's surrounded by a yellow circle. As we walk closer, a small glowing keypad rises from the ground. Kira places her keycard in the slot and types in a code. I try to see what the code is that she's typing, but her arm blocks my view. Suddenly the ground beneath our feet starts to lower itself as the elevator goes down. Dark, gloomy walls are all we can see through the glass tube. I have to hold onto the sides to stop myself from falling over since I'm not the most coordinated of people. Once we reach the ground, the glass doors slide open, revealing the dark and empty tunnel. The damp smell still lingers in the air swirling throughout my senses. *Home sweet home.*

Mark and Dale walk off together down the tunnel, playfully

shoving each other. As I watch them leave, I notice Dale looking back over his shoulder. I turn around to see what's caught his attention, but there are just dark walls behind me. As I turn back around his blue eyes meet mine for a split second, but before I can start my irrational thinking Troy gently places a hand on my back and leads me back to our dorm. Kira winks at me and walks confidently back into her own dormitory full of girls. I sigh.

"You shouldn't have gone." Troy looks straight ahead. *What?*

"I didn't know where Kira was taking me," I answer, a little angry with his tone. *Is he scolding me? Who does he think he is?*

"Then you should've asked." He clenches his jaw tightly. *Who the hell is he to tell me what I should do?*

"Derrick will find out, you know," he warns, shaking his head.

"Is that a problem?" I walk a bit faster to keep up with him. I've come to realise that he speeds his pace up when he's tense.

"It's dangerous. Derrick has his eye on everyone." He turns to look at me with concern.

"I didn't do anything wrong," I say, defending myself, but he doesn't respond. After a few minutes we finally reach the doorway into the dormitory.

"I've got to check on some stuff. I'll see you." He takes one last look at my bleeding lip and walks off without a reply.

"Bye then," I say.

When I turn around the dorm is empty. *Well, that's weird.*

"Hey, girly. You up for some fun?" A familiar slimy voice comes from behind me. Spinning around, Lewis grabs me by the arm. Going all karate mode on him, I shove my elbow into his side which makes him cry out. I start to run, my footsteps thudding against the puddles on the floor. The end of the dormitory is a dead-end so I spin back around. Lewis has a slight smirk on his face, but his eyes are filled with irritation.

"You're quite a feisty one, aren't you?" He walks over to me slowly, knowing full well that he's got me cornered.

"What do you want?" I step backwards as far as I can go before hitting my back against the wall.

"Hmm… What do I want?" His playful tone mocks me. "Maybe I'll just lock the two of us in this one room all night. Think of all the fun we could have then." His eyebrows rise up and his playful smile is back again. I can feel my heart erratically beating as my eyes dart aimlessly around for an escape.

Lewis has finally caught up to me and stops just so the tips of our feet touch. I try to back away, to do anything, but I can't see a way out.

"Would you like that? We could get to know each other a little better." He runs a finger down my cheek.

"I think I already know you just fine," I say, through gritted teeth.

He laughs. "Oh, is that so?"

I just glare at him and soon his playful smile turns into anger.

"So I see my charm isn't having an effect on you?"

"It that what you call it?" I can't help but laugh a little.

"Fine, you want it that way, girly, then you're going to have to come with me. You'll soon learn that being with me is what you've always dreamt about." His lips curve up into a grin. *I sincerely doubt that.*

Suddenly he grabs my arm and pulls me towards the door. With me fighting against him all the way, he drags me through the dark tunnel.

"Where are we going?" I shout, fighting against his strong frame.

"You really think you can survive here? A skinny *bitch* like you? You're about to see what happens when Derrick isn't around to protect you." He raises an eyebrow, slightly amused.

"What are you talking about?" My eyes widen. I continue to

struggle against him, shouting out but nobody can hear me. He just smiles and drags me through the dome-shaped doors and into the training hall.

A boy walks past us. His body is bruised and beaten, two other boys holding him up. His head hangs low and his dark eyes are closed while they drag him away. My own eyes widen, watching him leave the room. A few other boys sit around the outside, with cuts and scrapes all over their bodies. *What's going on?* My heart beats faster with the more bruising and injuries I see. A crowd surrounds the big training ring in the middle of the room and inside stands Jason, a.k.a sword fighting champion. Everyone suddenly turns to look at me. *What the hell is going on?*

"Go on!" Lewis pushes me into the ring and I stumble forward, trying to keep my balance. As I look up, Jason stands before me. His muscular, toned chest and his striking good looks immediately intimidate me. He narrows his eyes and holds out his sword, ready. *If you've never had a six foot, giant wall of muscles standing before you, you don't know what the word terrified means.* Just the way the coolness of his eyes wash over me, I get the feeling that he wants me dead. A slight prickle stings the back of my neck. The prickle that tells me to run, to escape. *What am I doing here anyway? Are they trying to make me fight this guy?*

"Come on, Ella. He's much less scarier than one of those nasty monsters out there!" Lewis laughs, now standing amongst the crowd gathered around the ring. No doubt trying to get his revenge because his charm didn't work on me.

The huge, metal bars around the edge seal us in. There is no way out of here without someone raising the bars. Jason's red face is full of anger and he snarls his teeth at me. *Charming.* My eyes widen as I look for another escape, I really don't want to have to fight. I search around hastily for a way out, but I can't find one. *Why are they forcing me to do this?* Jason suddenly runs at me, holding his sword in his right hand, but I dodge him and everyone laughs.

"Don't be afraid, girly!" Another voice taunts me.

I'm not afraid. I'm petrified. My heart beats rapidly, thudding inside of me. I continue to look for a way out but Jason runs at me again with fire burning in his eyes. *Fine*. They want me to fight, I'll fight.

He lunges for me and I hold my sword out in front, blocking him. I get a burst of adrenaline and I push him away using all my strength, and knee him in the leg. His eyes flare red as he catches me off guard. He grabs my arm, bending it backwards until I scream out. The icy fire flares through each vein until he lets go. I take the searing pain and slam my elbow into his side. I'm quite taken aback by my self-defence skills, but all that wrestling with Henry growing up really made me strong. Jason holds his hand to his side in surprise. Whilst he's distracted, I knee his leg and drive my heel into his foot. He lets out a loud roar of pain. *I have really pissed him off now.* I smile to myself. He lunges for me again, pushing me to the floor while I hold him off using my sword. My body shakes, using all my strength to fend him off. Beads of sweat have formed around my hairline because I am fighting with everything in me.

"You little tramp," he spits.

For a second, I'm totally startled by his words but it doesn't last long. *That's it*. Nobody calls me that! A sudden idea flashes through my head. The same idea I had when Robin Hutchins tried getting it on with me at my school prom, the same idea I had when he'd told the whole school that he'd gotten to third base with me the same night.

I bring my knee up and kick Jason straight in the groin. He closes his eyes in pain and surprise. I then whip the handle of my sword around and hit the side of his head. Cheap shot, but it worked. I stand up quickly, ready for him to respond, but he lays on the ground with his hand between his legs. I walk over and slam my sword into the ground, just missing his face.

"Don't *EVER* call me a tramp again!" He looks up at me, stunned, as does every other face in the room. With that, I walk out of the ring and a blonde-haired boy opens the metal bars for me. I don't look back while I slide my sword back into its case. They messed with the wrong girl.

As I walk back towards my dorm, my eyes feel heavy and tired. *Time to get some rest.* As I continue through the gloomy, endless tunnel I can start to hear a few footsteps following me. I'm really not in the mood for anything else right now. They get louder and louder, shaking the ground as I attempt to hide behind the nearest wall. But it's too late, they've already seen me. The two soldiers march in my direction. They both grab each of my arms and drag me down the tunnel.

"Ouch! Where am I going now?" I shout, squirming in their clutch. All I want to do is get some rest.

"Just shut up and come with us," one of them says, gripping my arm even tighter. I wince in pain. I have no strength left at all after that fight. They both shove me through a door on my left and slam it behind me. *Well, this feels just like my first day here.* I roll my eyes at the thought.

"Ella." A knowing voice comes from behind me. I spin around ready to attack, but find Derrick sitting in an old armchair, staring at me in amusement. The little room looks like an office. Stacks of books and old blueprints fill the shelves around the room and a warm smell of soup wafts through the air. The desk in front of him is filled from head-to-toe with jumbles of notes and lined paper.

When I take a better look around, I see a roaring fire to the side and a basket of coal by his feet.

"Take a seat." He smiles at me.

I walk over slowly and narrow my eyes taking, the seat opposite him.

"Why am I here?" I ask, confused.

"I hear some of our soldiers are leading you astray. You went out without my permission." He states it as a fact, not a question. His short-sleeved top reveals another tattoo on his arm, the letter 'L' surrounded by a dark yellow circle. It's the same symbol as outside. *How odd.* He has a few more grey hairs than the last time I saw him, so obviously being in charge is quickly aging him.

"I d-didn't…"

"You're lucky you're not dead!" he says, looking disgusted. "You're not properly trained and do not have the survival skills needed to stay alive out there." He raises his voice a little and it's starting to aggravate me. I quickly notice an old paperweight holding down a few notes that are scribbled across a piece of torn paper and I look at it with curiosity.

"I'm here now," I say, dragging my gaze away and looking him straight in the eye.

"By some stroke of luck, you are," he mumbles under his breath. The image of throwing the paperweight at his head quickly enters my mind, but I shake it away.

"What would your parents say?" He raises his eyebrows.

"My parents are dead." I narrow my eyes. *Where is he going with this?*

"Rebecca and James Holbert, am I correct?" He hides a smile. *Did he know my parents?*

"How do you know that?" I ask, trying to put two and two together.

"I know a lot more than you think I do." He just simply smiles and starts to write on a piece of paper in front of him.

"How did you know them?"

"I still know them now. They are part of The Society, Ella." He shakes his head in disgust.

"What's that?" *What the hell is he talking about? The Society, what is that?*

"You have no idea child, do you?" He glares at me. "Your parents knew about the disease spreading but they still stayed at home. Why?" He pulls at my memories.

I shrug, not understanding.

"They put you all in danger. They knew what was going to happen and they needed someone on the inside. Someone they knew and trusted, someone like you." He narrows his eyes at me. *Someone like me?*

"I don't understand." I look up with complete confusion on my face.

"They needed a reason to come find us. They want power, Ella. They will track every surviving civilisation down and take over..." His voice trails off as he starts pacing the room.

"The Society wants power?" None of this makes any sense.

"Yes, your parents wouldn't have died from an attack. They knew what was coming and prepared for it." He sighs, looking at me with his dark expression.

"They died. They died in front of me. I saw it!" I say, standing up.

"That's what they wanted you to believe, Ella. They're probably still alive." His eyes darken and a knock at the door startles me. Derrick raises his head at the sound.

"Stay safe, Ella." He gestures toward the door. "Don't stray from our training here. We don't want you getting into any more trouble now, do we?" I swear I see a smirk on his face, hiding under the dim light, but I can't be sure.

"We will talk later." He lowers his voice. I glare at him as I walk out of the door, passing the two soldiers on the way out. My parents can't still be alive. They died in front of me. I saw it with my own eyes. How dare he accuse them of working for The Society? But how much do I really know? I may not have known my own parents at all. Does that mean that Henry and Leila could still be alive? I shake my head, pushing the small flicker of hope away.

CHAPTER 8

THE LIGHTS FLICKER ABOVE ME, buzzing with little effort to stay awake. My weak footsteps echo down the tunnel. My eyelids are becoming heavier by the second and I find myself holding onto the walls to keep myself up straight. I need to get some rest. The day has completely worn me out. I miraculously find the entrance to the dorm room after several minutes of walking around aimlessly in the dark, with only the buzzing lights to keep me company. As soon as I enter the doorway everyone turns to look at me. I don't get any sly comments or any rude remarks as I make my way towards my bed. Even Lewis seems to be leaving me alone. It's when I take a seat on the edge of my bed that I see Terry, George, and Jim walking over to me.

"Hey, Ella. You were awesome earlier." Terry smiles brightly with a hint of a blush outlining his pale cheekbones. His curly brown hair lops over to the side as he takes a seat next to me. George sits on my other side and wraps an arm around my shoulder. I'm not used to warm gestures like this and the feeling throws me slightly.

"You sure can handle yourself," George laughs.

"You should've seen Jason's face when you left the ring." Jim's dark hair falls into his face, blocking his striking eyes that watch George's hand around my shoulder carefully.

"He just made me angry." I shrug.

"No one's going to mess with you anymore, that's for sure." George nudges me in the arm. "I never knew you were that tough."

I just laugh.

"Where did you go after you left anyway? We tried to find you, to see if you were alright." Jim looks at me with a concerned expression.

"Derrick wanted to see me." I shrug.

"Why?" Terry asks, looking confused.

"Something about The Society," I murmur.

"Not that again." George rolls his eyes. "The Society is just a load of crap."

"Says you." Jim raises an eyebrow at him.

"What's The Society?" I ask.

"It's this so-called group of people. They supposedly knew about the virus spreading and built underground facilities to help save humanity. Apparently it's surrounded by a huge iron gate in the middle of nowhere," Jim replies.

"Like this one?" I gesture around.

"Yes, but The Society is harder to find. Apparently they do a lot of experiments there. They are trying to find a cure to the virus attack."

"Really?" My voice squeaks a little higher than it was supposed to come out.

"Yeah they're looking for a cure but…" Jim gets cut off by the bell above us ringing. All the boys start to walk over to their beds.

"Guess that's time to sleep then." George rolls his eyes.

"I can't wait to get out of here," Terry mumbles under his breath as they all walk over to their own beds.

"See ya, Ella!" They all call from over their shoulders.

I awaken to a scream. A piercing scream that echoes through the air. I sit bolt upright in bed. The lights have all gone out around us so I can barely see a thing. I rub my eyes and lay my head back down on my pillow. *Maybe I just imagined it.* I start to drift off when I hear another scream followed by loud gunfire. *Okay, I didn't imagine that one.* I lift the covers off myself and pull on my boots. Looking around, no one else has been startled from the noise and Troy's bed is empty once again. *Doesn't he ever sleep?* I shake the thought away as I hear running footsteps echoing down through the tunnel outside the door.

Letting my blonde hair cascade down past my shoulders, I grab my jacket. Slowly I start to walk down the dorm room past all the sleeping guys, trying not to wake anyone up as I edge closer to the door. A boy starts to snore to my left, which causes me to jump slightly and silently curse to myself. I move closer and closer to the exit, hearing more running footsteps from outside. When I finally pull on the door handle, it creaks open and I hold my breath from the noise it makes, praying that no one has heard me get up. Peeking my head around the door, no one seems to be there. Only a few lights are switched on above me, but it's just enough to see where I'm going. Closing the door quietly behind me, I stand against the dark metal wall.

A few more screams fill the air, forcing a chill to run up my spine. Whatever's going on can't be good. I creep down the tunnel slowly, staying in the dark just in case I get caught out of bed. Who knows what Derrick will do if he catches me? The damp water drips from the ceiling, masking the noise of my boots. I tread as lightly as possible, hoping that no one hears. Suddenly a loud gunshot goes off and the ground rumbles beneath me. My heart beats faster since my adrenaline has now seriously kicked in. I start to walk faster towards the sound. I know it's a stupid thing to do, but I need to know what's going on.

Another gunshot goes off, a louder, more terrifying sound than the last. More footsteps behind me thud down the tunnel while I stand flat against the wall, hiding in the shadows. The footsteps become louder, running at a fast pace. The soldiers finally reach me and speed past, holding out their weapons. They suddenly disappear down the tunnel ahead.

"Hey," a quiet voice startles me. I turn around to see no one. My eyes widen, waiting to see who it is. *Have I been caught? Are they going to kill me?* I get ready to defend myself.

"Hey, it's me," Kira whispers, stepping out of the shadows. My heart rate immediately slows down, and I let out the sharp intake of air I've been holding in.

"Hey," I reply quietly, staying alert.

"Do you know what's going on?" Kira looks concerned.

"No, do you?"

She shakes her head and we hear another lot of screams, so we back further into the shadows.

"Right, you go that way and I'll go this way." She points in two different directions that the noise could be coming from. I nod as we hear more running footsteps coming towards us. We both immediately slam back against the cool sting of the wall. Four soldiers run past, carrying their large machine guns. Gleaming swords hang from their belts and they have straps of bullets hung over their broad chests. Kira looks at me, raising an eyebrow.

"Split up," she whispers, running ahead.

I go the opposite way and run towards the noise, following the soldiers. I don't even want to think about the gunshots. Surely soldiers wouldn't murder other survivors, but I'm not so sure anymore. Suddenly an arm grabs me out of nowhere and I start to scream, but a large hand covers my mouth and pulls me into a room on my left. I fight and kick, trying to break free, but the firm clutch my attacker has is too strong. A few lights switch on around us and I find myself back in the little training room Kira took me to the day before.

"Let go!" I shout through clenched teeth.

"Ella, calm down." A deep voice comes from behind me and my attacker lets me go. I immediately turn around to find Troy staring at me in bewilderment. *Does he not think grabbing me in the dark is slightly crazy?*

"Thank God you're okay." He looks out of breath and rather worried.

"Why, what's going on?" I ask, my heart beating faster.

"We've got to get out of here." His brown eyes meet mine with panic igniting in them.

"Why, what's wro…"

"Ella, we need to get out of here!" He comes over and grasps my shoulders. I meet his gaze but his expression looks distant, almost terrified.

"Not until you tell me what's wrong!" I demand.

He runs a hand through his hair while he paces up and down. Sighing, he looks me over in curiosity. I feel a jolt of electricity flow between us as soon as our eyes meet. A sudden pull of emotion. I soon scold myself and shake the feeling away.

"One of those things, those creatures, got in." He closes his eyes and shakes his head in disgust.

"What? How?" My eyes widen in shock. Maybe we're not safe

here. If one can get in, what's stopping the rest? Is that what Troy is trying to tell me? Is that why we need to go?

"It attacked a whole dormitory." His face looks pained.

"Are they, okay?" I ask. But it is a stupid question, because I already know they aren't going to be okay.

He shakes his head. "They're all gone."

He walks toward me once again. "We need to get out of here. If one of those creatures can get in, then what's stopping more from attacking us?" He looks at me for a reaction.

"But we can't just…leave. Where would we go?"

"We need to get somewhere safe, and the only place I can think of is The Society." He holds a hand to his head and lets out an intake of air.

"Why there?"

"They're trying to find a cure, right?" He raises an eyebrow.

"That's what I've heard," I shrug. But does he even know where to look?

"We need to head north. I have a rough idea where it might be, but it's a long journey. We would have to leave at night so no one spots us." He leans against the wall next to me.

"Who's we?"

"Anyone who wants to get out of here."

CHAPTER 9

"WE NEED TO LEAVE. I can't stand the thought of being here. I can't stand the thought of you being..." He stops himself and smacks the wall using his fist. *We do need to get out of here, but I doubt we'll be able to survive on our own.*

"We need a group of people to come with us. We'll have a better chance of survival out there with a group," I tell Troy, looking him straight in the eye. He considers this for a moment and then nods.

"You're right. We need a group, but we need to leave soon." His gaze lifts to mine and I can't seem to drag myself away. There is something underneath that strong exterior he hides behind. "I'll walk you back," he says, opening the door. Peeking our heads around the doorway, we hear a few voices coming from afar.

"Who's tha..." Suddenly Troy wraps his arm around my waist, covering my mouth with his hand and I gasp in surprise. *Damn it, he needs to stop doing that.*

"Shh," he whispers. When he pulls me into him, I can feel his muscular chest and the heat from his body. Butterflies start to dart around furiously in the pit of my stomach as I hold in a sharp intake of air. I feel his own heartbeat racing from within in his chest, and for a moment, I'm relieved that it's not just me feeling like this.

I'm snapped out of my little daydream when we hear the voices coming closer from outside. Slowly, we both peer around the door. Three soldiers dressed in dark uniforms are armed with guns and swords. They walk by us, dragging bodies behind them. I look up at Troy in shock but his eyes are fixated on the innocent victims in front of us. Turning my head back around, I get a glimpse of the young, brave survivors. They made it here, they survived the outside world, for what? To be killed?

As I watch the victims being dragged away I notice white, pale spots invading their skin as they hang lifelessly. My head starts to spin with memories of Leila. My breathing speeds up and my heartbeat starts to thump even harder. I clench my eyes shut when I suddenly see Leila standing there with tears running down her cheeks, her skin growing paler by the second. Her little eyes filled with horror and the terrified expression that stings my heart. My eyes start to well up, so I close them. Troy suddenly let's go of me as the soldiers disappear around the corner. Feeling like the world is ending, I crumble to the floor. All I can see is Leila's scared little face. I couldn't save her. There was nothing I could do. My head starts to pound as a pain slices through my heart. A single tear escapes, running down my trembling cheeks.

"Ella, look at me." Troy kneels down and brings my chin up to face him. "Ella, it's a shock, I know."

I try to shake away the hurt, the pain, and the loss, but it will not go away. The feelings will always be there. I can't just forget. *Stay strong, Ella.* I have to do this. I have to get away from here. I have to save as many others as possible.

"When do we leave?" I ask, surprising him. I will try to block out my pain, try to overcome the hurt of losing my family. I will fight with everything in me not to let this happen to others.

"Tomorrow night." He narrows his eyes. I nod and stand up.

"You okay?" Troy examines me.

"I'm fine." I brush off the dirt from my trousers. "Let's get back." I start to head for the door but Troy holds me back so he can go first.

"You're something else, Ella, you know that?" His last words were more of a mumble and I'm not sure if I even heard him correctly, but once the coast is clear we head on back down the tunnel.

Finally we make it back to the dorm to find everyone sitting up in bed. All eyes glare at us when we walk through the door.

"What the *hell* is going on?" one guy asks.

"You didn't go on a shooting spree…did you, girly?" Another guy looks wary of us. I sigh and walk over to my bed. They can't expect me to sleep, knowing that those creatures, those zombies, can get in here, can they?

"It's okay, I'll stay awake and watch out. Get some rest, Ella." Troy watches me carefully and I nod. When my head immediately hits the pillow, I can't help but drift off to sleep.

"Ella!" A voice wakes me. "There you are!" I open my sleepy eyes and find Kira running up the dorm towards me. Looking around, I notice all the beds are empty except mine. "Did you find out what happened?" She raises her eyebrows, waiting for the full story.

"I didn't see much, a few soldiers caught me sneaking around." She carries on and drops her eyes to the floor. I rub my eyes and catch a glimpse at her arms. They are covered in bruises, large bruises in the shape of handprints.

"Are you okay?" I ask.

"Yeah, I'll be fine. They just wanted to teach me a lesson." She rolls her eyes. "So, what happened with you?" She awaits my answer, taking a seat on the edge of my bed. I slowly sit up, stretching my back, and lean against the headrest.

"A zombie got in." I break the news to her.

"WHAT?!" She jumps off the bed in shock.

"They attacked a whole dorm."

"Oh, God. It's happening. We need to get out of here, Ella. We need to go!" She jumps up and tries to pull me out of bed.

"Whoa, we're planning to leave."

"Who's *we*?" She raises an eyebrow.

"Me." Troy walks over, carrying a tray of food. Kira turns her head around and narrows her eyes at Troy.

"*You* are coming with us?"

"I think you'll find that *you* are coming with *us*." He hides a smirk under his blank expression as Kira rolls her eyes again.

"When do we leave?" she asks excitedly.

"Tonight," I reply.

"Here." Troy puts the tray in front of me. It is filled with cereal and bread.

"Thanks."

"I'll round up a few more guys and we can meet tonight then." She starts to walk off. "Meet you at the elevator at midnight," Kira calls from over her shoulder. She dismissively waves her hand as she walks out of the dorm.

Troy sits on his own bed and watches me eat, not saying a word.

"Troy, can I ask you something?" I say, between mouthfuls. He raises his eyebrows awaiting my question.

"Derrick will know where to look for The Society, won't he?" He looks slightly shocked at my question, but then thinks it over and slowly nods. Right. Then I know what I have to do.

I knock at the steel, metal door in front of me.

"Ella, what do I owe the pleasure?" Derrick opens the door and gestures for me to come inside his little office. I don't waste any time when he shuts the door behind us.

"How do you know my parents?" My gaze burns into him and he looks quite taken aback by my presence.

"Ella…" he starts.

"The truth," I snap.

"Why don't you take a seat?" He pulls out an armchair for me to sit on. His office is messier than the last time I was here. His eyes also have dark lines underneath them and his hair is tousled, as if he has been running his hands through it all night.

"Your parents work for The Society," he simply replies.

"I don't know what that means."

He sighs. His tired gaze meets mine.

"You must know something about The Society by now, child — what with all the whispering in this place." He cocks his head to the side.

"I heard that they're trying to find a cure," I say.

He nods slowly and picks up a pen.

"They are a secret Society. They've hidden themselves away so they can no longer be found. They knew the virus attack was coming. They knew what was going to happen." He shakes his head in disgust.

"So, why didn't they do something?"

"That's what I'm trying to work out. Why didn't they do something? Why did they go into hiding? Why did they do absolutely nothing?" He runs his hand through his dishevelled grey hair and I sigh.

"All I know is that your parents are somewhat involved with them. I was too. When I got too curious, they removed me. I ended up here. A safe house underground for all survivors." He starts writing.

"You were a part of them?" I ask, surprised.

"Yes, but I don't remember much. It's like my memories have been wiped out." He shakes his head again.

"Like I said. Your parents may still be alive. That's all I know." He rises from the desk. I guess that's all I'm getting from him for now. I don't think pushing him for any more answers will get me anywhere, so I just nod and walk over to the doorway.

Derrick hands me a piece of paper as he opens the metal door for me. I look down and find a roughly drawn map.

"Be careful." He gives me a knowing look and with that, he shuts the door. How did he know we were leaving? Did he know? Or did he just guess?

I look down to find a drawn guide of the direction and the destination to head in. Troy was right. We need to head north.

I walk back down the tunnel, passing room by room. I stop at a door on my right. The rusty, metal frame has been marked with the letter 'L' and the familiar yellow circle surrounds it. I look down the tunnel for a sign of anyone sneaking up on me, but it is all clear so I edge closer to the door and peer into the room. All the beds are empty but as I look closer, I see that the walls are coated with blood — green diseased blood that covers every wall. Blood is spread along the floor and stops just before the doorway. Obviously people were trying to escape, but didn't make it out in time. The disturbing smell oozes out of the room so I hold my hand over my nose. I shut the door to stop the horrid smell traveling further down the tunnel.

Slowly I lean against a wall, thinking, trying to process the escape tonight. Are we going to survive? What if someone gets bitten? If one zombie can attack an entire dorm here then we will be safer out there, trying to find The Society. I might find my parents if Derrick is telling the truth. I hope they are still alive, but a little voice inside my head knows that there is a very slim chance. I just hope that when we do get there it won't be a wasted journey. I hope they have more survivors and are trying to find a cure to this horrible virus. I close my eyes to take in everything, but I start to hear voices coming from behind the wall I lean on.

I crease my brows at the sound. *Who is that?* I hear even more muffled voices as I lean closer. I can just about make out what is being said while I lean my head up against the steel, cold metal and listen to the echoing voices.

"Yes…I know…the girl's sister. Yes…alive…in experiments…" The male voice crackles and it's hard to hear.

Who are they talking about? I lean in closer, pressing my ear as far as it will go.

"The… girl…Ella…yes…here…under…watch…Society… yes…" The voice starts to fade out but I try to listen harder.

"They're…coming… don't…mess…up…no…don't…"

"Hey! What are you doing?" A loud voice comes from behind me. I spin around to find two soldiers marching towards me. *Oh great.*

"I said, what do you think you're doing?" The taller one glares at me. They're both dressed in dark, black armour and each carry a rather large gun.

"I-I was just on my way back…"

"Yeah right. Of course you were." They shorter one rolls his beady little eyes. I immediately take a disliking to him.

"Do we have to teach another one of you a lesson?" one of them says, laughing. They must mean Kira. I remember the bruising on her arm and I gulp.

"We really showed that girl last night." The other laughs with the taller one.

That's it! How dare they hurt Kira? I don't think twice as I immediately bring my knee up and kick the taller one between his legs. His shocked expression doesn't last long and he closes his eyes in pain, holding himself in agony. The shorter one is already aiming a gun at me and he marches in my direction. Maybe that wasn't the best idea in the world. The soldier aiming for me has venom in his eyes. He pulls back the trigger slowly and I get ready to run. My mother always said: *"A running target is harder to hit."*

Suddenly from nowhere Kira runs at him and knocks the gun to the floor. She holds him by his shirt and pushes him to the ground. She has the element of surprise as Mark and Dale pop up from the dark shadows and hold the two soldiers down.

"Don't mess with us!" Kira spits at the two soldiers. She picks up the gun from the floor and throws it at me. I quickly catch it and look up at her.

"Thanks," she smiles. "You may need that for tonight." She gestures to the gun in my hand. I nod and hide it in the waistband of my trousers. I look up to find Mark and Dale teaching the soldiers a lesson of their own.

"What's that?" She points to the piece of paper in my pocket.

"Oh, Derrick gave it to me." I hand it to her and she examines it.

"Is this what I think it is?" she asks.

"Yeah," I nod.

"Why did he give this to you?"

I shrug, not knowing what to say. She thinks it over for a little while and then hands it back to me.

"Strange." She furrows her brows.

"I heard someone talking when those two found me," I mumble, gesturing towards the unconscious soldiers.

"What do you mean?" she asks, taking me to the side.

"They were talking to someone. They said my name and something about someone's sister. Oh, and something about experiments too." I look up and I realise how crazy I must sound. Kira doesn't say a word as she scans my worried face.

"How odd." She continues to look confused.

"What's odd?" Mark saunters toward us, putting an arm around Kira's shoulder. She rolls her eyes and shoves him away.

"Nothing. Let's get ready." She gives me a knowing look and we all head back to the dorms.

CHAPTER 10

ALL THE BEDS ARE STILL empty. According to Kira, everyone has been in extra training today due to the attack last night. Derrick wants everyone to be on high alert. I use the opportunity to change my clothes. I grab a pair of leather trousers with a few pockets in the side, attaching a grey belt so I can keep my sword on me at all times. As I pull on the black trousers, they cling to what few curves I have. Next I grab a black top that matches and pull it over my head. In addition, I also grab my boots, doing up the laces and tucking in the bottom of my trousers. Finally I grab my black waterproof jacket and tug it on as I head out of the dorm, picking up a small backpack on the way. I walk towards the little training room and find Troy already waiting there for me.

"Here." He hands me a small knife and my eyes widen, looking at the sharp blade. I gently push it into the little case and slide it into my biggest pocket.

He then grabs a gun and a knife of his own, double-checking his sword is attached to his belt. I make sure I have my own sword and the gun Kira picked off one of the soldiers earlier. Troy turns around to face me and I'm immediately drawn to his muscular chest. His leather top clings to every hill and curve of his body, but he ruins the moment by tugging his jacket over the tight clothing.

"Take these." He hands me a few cans of food, snapping me out of my daydream. I put them in my backpack. He also hands me a compass from the shelf behind him and I find an 'E' engraved onto the back of the silver gadget. I look up and find him hiding a soft smile on his lips and I can feel my cheeks slightly flushing.

To top off all of the necessities we need to survive, he then hands me a small blanket and a few bottles of water. After loading everything into my backpack, I thank him and when we finally have everything we need, we sneak down the tunnel towards the elevator. Looking to our left and right, we check to see if we've been caught, but everyone is still in the training room. Kira, Mark, and Dale all wait for us at the elevator and I suddenly feel guilty for leaving the others behind. As we walk towards Kira, I see George, Terry, and Jim walking over to us down another tunnel, each with a backpack of their own.

"Didn't think you were leaving without us, did you?" George grins at me and I laugh.

"Alright, you all ready?" Kira keeps her voice down as we all climb into the circular walls of glass. I take a long, last look at the underground tunnels and await the adventure before us.

When we reach the cool breeze of damp air, we all climb off the elevator one by one. The twinkling stars fill the night sky and the moon looms over us. The wind caresses my cheeks, flowing through my long, blonde hair. I hold my jacket tighter around me while Kira and Dale get out their flashlights."Right, we've got two trucks and two people who know how to drive." Kira stands upright, entering take-charge mode, gesturing towards Dale and Troy.

"George, Terry, and Jim will go with Troy. Me, Ella, and Mark will go with Dale," Kira announces. Troy looks like he's about to argue with her, but sensing his scowl, Kira takes my arm and heads off towards our truck, not giving him a chance to respond. I look back over my shoulder to catch Troy's gaze meeting mine. His deep brown eyes watch me carefully as if it's the last time he's ever going to see me. I break the moment and climb into the passenger side of the first truck. We each have a black Land Rover. The back has four leather seats, two on each side. The windows have no glass and the roof has a gaping hole that lets in the cool air.

Dale starts up the truck and the other vehicle speeds off in front of us. I feel a sting of pain watching the others drive off, but I shake away the strange feeling and turn my attention back towards our group. Dale turns on the dim headlights and follows the others. This is it. No turning back.

The shimmering nightfall fills the sky. The cool wind wraps around us, sending a chill down my spine. It's feels good to be out in the open air — even if it is filled with zombies roaming around.

"How did a zombie get inside?" I snap my head around to ask Kira. She thinks it over for a minute and looks to Mark. He shakes his head and shrugs.

"I really don't know, Ella. It either got in by itself, which I find very unlikely, or someone let it in, which I don't understand." He shakes his head in defeat.

"Why would anybody want to let one of those things inside?" I ask the question that's been whirling around in my mind for the last half an hour.

"I don't know, Ella," Kira replies, smiling sympathetically.

Why would anybody want to put others at risk like that? I don't understand. Even if it did get in by itself, *how* is the question?

"They're not very smart, zombies," Dale says from the driver's seat. His jet-black hair catches the moonlight.

"What do you mean?" I ask.

"I mean, they're not very smart. They usually travel around in a small group and can smell human blood from a mile away. They're attracted to it. They never have plans of attack, they're just drawn to fresh meat." Dale keeps his eyes on the road.

"Fresh meat?" My hands start to shake.

I look out of the small window next to me to see the other truck a few meters ahead. The headlights beam out in front of them to see what's ahead.

"Doesn't the light attract zombies?" I ask whoever is listening.

"Yes, but we can't see what's ahead without it," Mark smirks. "Anyway, we should get some sleep. I'm knackered." He yawns.

"Me too." Kira starts to lay her head down on the seat. Mark starts to cuddle in next to her, but Kira shoves him away.

"Just because I'm drowsy, doesn't mean you can take advantage." She pulls out her gun and effortlessly aims it towards Mark. I laugh as Mark finds another place to rest his head.

"Worth a shot," he mumbles.

I don't feel tired in the slightest, so I just sit and enjoy the soft breeze whisking over my pale skin. I wrap my jacket around me tighter, trying to keep warm, and gaze back out the truck window. I can't see much since it is pitch-black outside, so I just enjoy the sensation of being in the night air. Every now and again we go past a few fireflies that dance through the night, sparkling blue fireflies that take my breath away. Suddenly, the headlights of the truck in front go out.

"What th…" Dale brakes and our truck comes to a complete stop. Kira and Mark both jump up in alarm, Mark curses out loud after hitting his head against Kira's. Kira shoves him hard, holding her own head in pain.

A few shouts come from in front of us as we all watch in anticipation. Seconds tick by while we watch for any movement, any sense of what's going on. Flashes of terror quickly run through my mind, but I shake them away. Deciding I can't take the dreaded silence any longer, I quickly grab our flashlight and shine it around... but we still can't see anything. I hear a few low growls. Nothing normal would make that sound — it almost sounds...inhuman. Another high-pitched echo runs through the air, causing Kira and Mark to both hold out their weapons.

"What the *hell* is going on?!" Mark yells.

"I don't know." I shine the flashlight about, but still can't find what's wrong.

Another few shouts and screams can be heard from outside. I climb out of the truck and hold the flashlight out in front of me. I know it's not the smartest thing to do, but Kira jumps out and joins me. I take small, gradual steps, edging closer to the noise. My heart beats faster with every second, waiting for something to jump out. I shine the flashlight around, but all I find is the dusty ground we now walk on.

"Where the hell is the other truck?" I whisper.

"I don't know," Kira replies, holding out her sword and ready for an attack. Dale and Mark start up the engine behind us and start to scan the area with the headlights on.

The shouts and screams have stopped. It's pure silence as we edge forward. I put my hand on my sword, ready to fight whatever's out there. But nothing. I keep walking forwards. The truck shouldn't be this far away.

We keep walking, waiting for death to find us.

The truck Dale drives stops just ahead of me and Kira. I sigh because it is clear they haven't found anything. Suddenly the headlights go out on the second truck and Mark screams. I immediately widen my eyes and look to Kira. She gives me a worried expression as we both dart towards the noise. We near the truck and I stop dead in my tracks, hearing a low growl rumbling behind me. Spinning around, I shine my flashlight to catch a zombie heading for Kira, its deadly teeth snapping at her heels. As my heart beats rapidly in alarm, I run at the monster with every single inch of me flaming with rage.

I grab my sword and in one quick motion I stab the creature straight through the heart. Kira spins around to see the zombie lying at her feet and looks up gratefully. After wiping off the end of my blade on the dusty ground, we continue to run over to the screams. Dale shouts out and we speed up our pace, running as fast as we can possibly go.

A few growls suddenly circle us. I shine my flashlight around but there are no creatures in sight. I thought they weren't very smart? I thought they wouldn't have a plan of attack? *Obviously we were wrong.* Kira continues to run forwards, but I stop to listen. Heavy breathing comes from behind me. I shine my light into a horrific face creeping towards us. Terry's face is covered in white spots and his eyes are filled with fiery venom. His body is as pale as snow as he runs at us. His skin is slowly starting to detach from his face while the deathly smell radiating from him lingers within the air.

"Terry? What are you doing?"

Another body flies at him, knocking him to the ground, and Terry lets out an inhuman roar of pain. There is nothing left of him. Terry's gone because of me. He could still be alive if we hadn't escaped. Troy stands in front of me pulling his sword out from Terry's diseased body.

"I c-can't…I d-don't…" I stutter, trying to find some words.

Any words. But nothing.

"He was bitten." Troy looks up at me, unsure of my reaction, either waiting for me to go off the rails or break down and cry. But I do neither. All I can do is stare at him. "He shouldn't have turned that fast. The virus is obviously a lot stronger than we thought." Troy walks over to me slowly, as if his presence will suddenly startle me, but I just continue to stand there, looking at Terry's body lying face down on the ground. I can't move.

He's dead. Dead because of us. Dead because of me. He should've stayed. He could still be alive. He didn't deserve that ending. Tears fill my eyes as they threaten the surface, trying to break through, but I don't cry. Seeing my hurt expression, Troy grabs my arm and forces me to turn away from Terry, but I can't. I can't just leave him here.

"Ella, we've got to move." Troy tugs at my arm.

"I can't!" I snap.

"Yes, you can." He cups my chin to face him. His clenched jaw is covered in a small amount of stubble, his skin covered with dark bruises and streaks of blood. He runs a hand through his dark brown hair as beads of sweat slide down the side of his face.

"We need to go, Ella." The determination is his eyes fill me with courage, so I start to run. Troy runs next to me and I feel comforted by his presence.

Mark screams again just ahead of us and we sprint even faster towards the sound. Kira suddenly comes back into view surrounded by three grotesque creatures. The blackened skin hangs from each horrific face as the raw bleeding stains the ground. I run at one of the zombies and slam my sword, taking off its head. I whisk around, taking out another and another. *Where are they all coming from?* Troy stands next to me, fighting, and plunges his sword into a zombie on his right. I watch it fall to the floor. He wipes off the end of his weapon and walks over to me.

"I think that's it, for now. Come on." He grabs my arm and Kira follows us over to the truck. When we get there, we find George and Jim waiting for us.

"We don't know where Dale and Mark are," George pants, clearly out of breath.

"Right, you go that way, we'll go this way," Troy shouts.

"No need." Dale comes into view, holding up Mark's body that looks badly injured.

"Has he been bitten?" Kira asks, nearly in tears.

"No, I got there in time. But he can't walk." Dale hangs his head. Troy walks over and helps drag Mark's body along.

"That's all of them, I think." Dale looks up to meet my gaze. We all nod but stay cautious.

"But we do need to get out of here."

Troy lifts Mark into the truck with Dale's help and we all climb in next to him, squeezing into the one vehicle. Troy and Dale climb into the front, and we all watch the sunrise. The truck hurls forward once again, leaving Terry behind.

CHAPTER 11

"I'M SORRY ABOUT TERRY." I look up to see George's and Jim's pained expressions.

"It's okay, it's not your fault." Jim smiles weakly.

"If I hadn't have let him come, if I…"

"Ella, he wanted to come. You wouldn't have been able to stop him. He wanted to get out just as much as you did." Jim cocks his head to the side.

"But I…"

"There was nothing you could've done, Ella." Kira sits next to me and puts an arm around my shoulders. Next to her sits Mark, leaning against her body, barely moving.

"Is he going to be okay?" I ask. George looks at me with a blank expression as Kira looks down at his shaking body.

"What happened back there anyway?" I ask.

"Well, we were driving along and out of nowhere something crashed into the side of the truck. Troy slowed down to see what it was, but as soon as he did, something collided with the front and knocked out the headlights." Jim shakes his head and George carries on.

"We tried to climb out, but we were surrounded. Those creatures broke the doors and held us by our throats. We all grabbed our swords and fought them off but…" George looks down at the floor. "Terry didn't stand a chance."

"Why? What happened to him?" My eyes start to water, but I hold it back.

"Two of them — *things* — grabbed his neck and dragged him out of the truck. By the time we got to him, it was too late. He was infected by the virus and his body was already turning pale." Jim nudges George in the arm, trying to cheer him up.

"I'm so sorry."

"Hey, it wasn't anyone's fault." Jim shrugs sympathetically.

"So he turned into one of them, just like that? It doesn't make any sense." Kira frowns.

"It normally takes a few hours for the virus to spread to the heart, so I don't understand."

Dale joins in from the driver's seat. "A few hours? How could Terry change into one of those monsters so fast?"

"I really don't know, the virus must be stronger than we thought. It's the only explanation." Kira shrugs.

I look out the back window and close my eyes, thinking of the innocent body we've left behind. Even though Terry was gone and a monster had taken over, I still feel guilty for leaving him.

"Do you want me to drive for a while?" Troy asks Dale. They stop the truck to swap over. The sun is almost out and the morning sunrise spreads over the rubble left on the ground. The warm orange and fiery red gently brush over the earth as a bright ball of light rises above the jagged mountains in the distance.

"We may as well look around here for any food or medicine."

Kira stands up, leaving Mark laying on the seat beside her.

"I'll go with you." I stand up and Dale stands too.

"We'll stay here and keep an eye on Mark." George looks at me, and I nod. Kira climbs out the back, and I follow. Dale joins us at the side of the truck.

"I'm going to see if I can find any kind of fuel for the truck." Troy runs a hand through his short hair. "It'll be completely out soon and we'll be walking if I don't find any." I watch him walk off and look around at the earth standing before me.

Surrounding us is a town. A worn down, empty town. Bits of crumbling, brick buildings remain and every tiny particle of life is covered with dirt. A rotten smell lingers in the air while we travel further into the streets. Each streetlight flickers with an eerie essence as the light travels through the misty fog loitering in the air, waiting to swallow its next victim. I silently pray that it won't be us. Rusty old cars are left deserted on the sides of the roads, most of them wearing deep claw marks on the doors. We look to see if we can find any keys to start up the engines, but most of them are broken and covered in dust.

Sprawled ligaments also litter the pavements and as I look at each one, it fills me with dread. Most of these people had families and homes. They didn't deserve this. No one deserves this. The upsetting emotions just make me more and more angry at the zombies. Tearing my life apart like that, tearing the earth apart. If I know one thing that's true, I will fight till the day I die, if that's what it takes. I will defend others from this nightmare. I will fight zombies no matter the cost and make them pay for what they did to my family.

As we continue to walk through the lonely streets, we spot a tall house to our left. Its windows are jagged and the red brickwork is smothered with green blood. But it seems to be the best house to check out so far. The damage is minimal and it may also hold food and medicine.

"Let's check in there." Dale points toward the house.

We walk cautiously through the torn-down doorway and find a kitchen to our left. The house is in a terrible state. Each room has ripped red curtains and dust spread everywhere, but I stop in the hallway when I spot a few small footprints on the floor. I bend down to have a closer look and Kira does the same.

"At least they look..." Her eyes widen. "...human."

"Yeah, but they look new, like someone's been here recently." I stand up and gulp, facing her. More survivors could either be a very good thing or a very bad thing. We wouldn't want them to think we're trespassing on their town. But at least there's hope for others still being alive.

After thinking it over, we follow the footprints into the kitchen. The whole place has been raided. The cupboard doors are open and each shelf is completely empty. The rotting smell coming from the fridge is definitely something we need to stay away from.

"Ugh. What is that smell?" Kira holds her nose.

"Probably your feet." Dale tries to hide a smirk. Kira turns her head around to scowl at Dale and slices his shoulder with the tip of her blade.

"Hey, watch it!" Dale hisses at her, but it only makes her grin even more.

Why Dale feels the need to wind Kira up is beyond me. There seems to be a past with these two, but I can't quite work it out. I get snapped out of my thoughts when Kira walks over to the fridge. As she opens the door, she jumps back in shock. "Eww!" She shivers.

Dale and I walk over to see a diseased zombie head placed on the middle shelf. Its eyes are dark and hollow with its mouth set wide open, as if it's just about to bite us. A warning, perhaps? "Talk about rotting food, that's disgusting."

Eventually, after the sight has dramatically scarred each of us for the rest of our lives, we close the door while holding our noses and walk out the kitchen. We're obviously not going to find any food in there. Kira leads us out the front door so we can go raid a few more houses, still not finding anything useful.

"What about that place over there?" Kira points to what looks like a factory of some sort. It's the biggest building around here and looks the most dangerous — a perfect place for zombies to be hiding. The perfect place to trap them. The roof is barely there anymore, with crumbling pieces of grey plaster falling onto the ground, and the outside walls stand tall. At least the glass windows are still intact.

"Come on, then." Dale leads the way as we travel towards it.

When we finally get to the door, we slowly push it open, as if waiting for the floor to cave in, or something to jump out of the shadows…but nothing. The whole place is dark, with only a little light shining through the small windows. The small, glistening patch of moonlight highlights the sheets covering most of the old equipment, as tiny cobwebs outline the beams holding up the ceiling. The air is damp and I shiver from the uneasiness. Rusty and beaten is the only way to describe this place.

"Right, split up. See what you can find." Dale takes the right and Kira goes upstairs. I take the few rooms on the left, shining my flashlight around, finding nothing but dust.

When I walk into the next room, I notice it's filled with cardboard boxes and a few metal pipes hang from the ceiling, with small sparks falling to the ground. I search around the cardboard boxes and open up each one. All I find are a few rats and spiders. They don't scare me like they used to. I don't even flinch. Instead, I just move them out of my way, searching for any food, or medicine for Mark. Nothing. I continue into the next room and find the same small footprints on the ground. Could someone have possibly cleared out this place too? The room is once again filled with boxes and metal pipes. I search around endlessly and it starts to aggravate me. I still find nothing.

I walk into the last room on this side of the building. There are more footprints on the floor leading to the corner of the room, which is piled high with cardboard. There's a big 'X' in front, made out of grey, metal pipes. I walk towards it, shining my flashlight around. I edge closer and climb through the pipes. Suddenly, a big metal cage falls down on top of me and I shout out, cursing. I silently wait for my attacker, breathing heavily but I see no one.

CHAPTER 12

"ANYONE HERE?" I SHOUT. "CAN you let me out?!"

No reply, except a small rustle from within the mass of cardboard in front of me. I squint my eyes, trying to search for any other movement. The cardboard begins to rustle again and I widen my eyes, waiting for a zombie to appear and kill me, waiting for my quick and painful death. Maybe being brutally murdered is the best way to die. There's no scale of time to wait for your slow death — the agonising rush would only last a few minutes, maybe even a few seconds. This is possibly how my loved ones felt, with their last few empty seconds of life. Henry lost everything, his caring and protective demeanour, his hopes and dreams, gone in one quick flash by him risking his life for me. His whole world spinning by as he lunged for the monster with his bare hands. Is this how he felt? He didn't wait, he didn't ponder. He fought right to the end. His spirit will live on and somehow I feel his presence within me, making me stronger. I start to feel a slight warmth on my shoulder, as if Henry's comforting me from afar.

I'm snapped back into reality when I hear another rustle, a louder more terrifying rustle. Whatever it is, it's getting closer. I slam my back against the cage surrounding me as the jagged edges pierce my skin. I yelp in surprise, looking down at the pointed arrows holding me in position, ready for my predator. The prison is cleverly made out of thin metal pipes that act as bars. Slyly moving my hand over the handle of my sword, I get ready for whatever's out there. Suddenly a small voice comes from inside the cardboard dome.

"You're not a monster, are you?" the sweet voice asks. *What the…?*

"Uh, no." I look closer at the boxes, trying to figure out where the small voice is coming from.

"Stay where you are! Do not move!" the tiny voice demands. I immediately freeze as a small glistening blade hurtles through the air, just missing my head. The knife slams into the wooden wall a few feet away and I gulp.

"Who are you?" the voice asks. I see a glimpse of red hair, the deep rich colour distracting me from the question.

"Answer me, intruder!" Another blade whisks through the air past my stomach. *Whoa!* That one almost hit me. Again, the knife slams into the wall next to the first one.

"M-my name is, Ella." I am feeling a little shaken from the knife throwing.

"What do you want, Ella?"

"I want to get out of here." I shake the bars of the cage.

Suddenly a small, pale face comes into view from within the boxes. A pretty young girl pokes her head out. Small freckles lay just above her flushed cheeks and her big brown eyes examine me. She doesn't look any older than nine years old. Her face scans me over. When she's completely satisfied that I'm not a zombie about to eat her, she lifts the cage up using a small rope. Narrowing her eyes at me, she waits, as if she's expecting me to attack her or something.

"You may come in." She turns around and crawls through the tunnel of boxes.

I walk over carefully and kneel down. *Who is this girl and why is she out here alone? Or is she alone?* That thought worries me. I start to crawl through the entrance of the cardboard dome, following her flowing red hair. When I crawl through the last box, I notice that it opens up into a little den. Sitting there is the little girl. She holds another knife up against the doorway and I immediately come to a stop.

"First, you need to answer some questions." She narrows her brown eyes once again.

"Okay," I reply, warily. No need to upset her, or I may just end up with a knife in my throat.

"How did you find me?" She gets straight to the point — no need to beat around the bush, I guess. I like her already.

"I was looking for food and I accidentally got caught in your trap," I answer. It seems to have satisfied her because she moves onto the next question.

"Do you have an army?" I can't help but smile a little at her questions.

"No, I don't have an army."

"Are you sure?"

"I'm quite sure."

She narrows her eyes once again and starts to lower the knife.

"Are you here alone?" I ask. *Big mistake.* Her grip on the knife hardens and her eyes fill with fear. She holds a shaky hand out at me again and I widen my eyes at her reaction.

"I'm asking the questions." She doesn't look amused. Just great. I have now successfully ticked off a nine-year-old.

"Are you carrying any weapons?" She raises an eyebrow.

"Yes," I sigh.

"Leave them at the door." She puts down the knife and makes room for me to crawl through the rest of the tunnel.

"Nice place you've got here," I say, looking around. A pile of food sits in the corner and cans of drink are scattered throughout the place. I think we've found our food thief.

The small cardboard room is about ten feet wide. She's cut out little stars in the ceiling and each one catches the moonlight from the outside windows. They create small, delicate shapes on the walls, almost like her own wallpaper of stars. I sit cross-legged on the floor, ducking my head to fit into the small space. The young girl looks up at me.

"Thank you. I made it myself." Her smile beams as her pale cheeks redden. She places the knife back in her pocket and seems to completely relax in her little place of confinement. "You're the first guest I've had." She giggles. Her red hair falls just past her skinny shoulder bones and she wears torn, old school clothes. Plaid red shorts, with what I'm guessing was a white top, that has become so dirty it's now stained with dry blood and dirt. The bold collar is dark blue, with a silver pin stuck on the side. She immediately catches me gazing at it.

"That's my school pin." She smiles and hands it to me. It has three arrows pointed upwards and a rope holding them all together. The pin fits perfectly within the palm of my hand.

"It's pretty." I hand it back and she smiles.

"My name's Zoe." She has a mischievous grin playing on her lips.

"Nice to meet you, Zoe," I say. "How did you end up in here?"

"Umm…there were those monsters everywhere, so Mummy and Daddy told me to run and hide and they would come find me. I ran in here and hid under these boxes. They never came. When I went back out after the monsters had gone, I saw them lying on the floor." Her little eyes look down at the ground.

"So you're here, by yourself?" I look around, raising an eyebrow.

"Yeah," she smiles. "Are you?"

"No, there are a few of us. We're traveling, trying to find The Society." I fiddle with a few rocks on the floor. She fidgets a little too, probably because I did tell her that I don't have an army, which is true, but she might think that I lied to her.

"The Society?" She cocks her head to the side.

"It's the safest place. They're trying to find a cure to the monsters. I think my parents..." I think about what I'm going to say and stop myself when I remember what she must be going through, losing her own parents that way.

"You think your parents might be there?" She looks up at me with a weak smile. I nod, feeling guilty.

"If I can find them." I shake away the hope.

"Can I come?" she asks, looking up with her big brown eyes. I don't like the idea of her coming along with us, but I don't like the idea of leaving her here on her own either. *Damn that puppy dog look she's giving me.*

"Yes, of course." I smile and she starts to get excited. She grabs a small handmade bag and starts packing up her food.

"Here." I hand her my backpack to pack some in.

"Thanks," she replies, tossing in a few tins. "Are you sure you're not a monster?" She narrows her eyes at me. I laugh and nod.

"I'm sure." I hold out my hand, but she neglects to take it. She just leads me out of the cardboard dome and back into the gloomy factory.

Kira and Dale are nowhere to be seen. They're probably still inside. I wonder if they've found anything. *What will they make of our newest group member?* We now stand outside the building, Zoe stands next to me in her torn and ripped clothing. She looks around and cautiously starts to crouch down.

"What's wrong?" I ask.

She puts a finger to her lips and gestures for me to crouch down next to her. She starts to move towards half a brick wall by the side of the burnt building. I follow her, keeping low to the floor. We start to hear a strange noise, a noise I can't place. We both hide behind the little brick wall, peering over the top slightly to see what's going on. Just then, we see a few men walk past. They all wear green uniforms with a large symbol on the back. The bold 'L' is surrounded by a thick yellow circle, the same symbol as I've seen at the Underground. Each soldier carries a gun on them while they all walk along together. They keep their eyes focused in front of them as if patrolling the area. So these must be the soldiers rescuing new survivors.

"They come here all the time," Zoe whispers.

"They do?" I ask, keeping my voice low as we watch them march past.

"They march through and kill people." Her big terrified eyes meet mine and I gulp. *Kill people?*

Peering over the half-built wall, I watch them walk away.

"What do you mean they kill people?" I sit down next to Zoe, keeping hidden in the shadows. She shrugs and stays quiet. We sit there in silence until Zoe eventually gives in and sighs. I do admire her stubbornness, and she sort of reminds me of…*No.*

Not going there. I cannot allow myself to think of her. It hurts too much.

"They killed another girl like me." Zoe's eyes are filled with terror. "They shot her in the street." Tears start to well up and glisten in the corners of her brown eyes.

"Zoe, I'm so sorry." I put a hand on her shoulder as she begins to cry.

"She was my friend," Zoe sobs. I continue to watch the soldiers walk towards the end of the street, turning a corner and eventually disappearing out of sight.

"I'm sorry." She wipes away her tears.

Why on earth would soldiers be killing innocent people? What would they gain from it? The questions float through my mind, traveling and spinning uncontrollably so that any rational answers are destroyed. None of this makes sense. I want the answers so bad that it hurts to think about it.

"It's okay, but we do need to get out of here, before they come back," I say, starting to stand up, but Zoe pulls me back down. Suddenly a loud gunshot goes off, breaking the deathly silence. My eyes widen and so do Zoe's as we both look at each other. We peek our heads back over the wall, but see nothing.

Zoe pulls at my jacket and urges me to follow her. She puts a small finger to her lips and starts to crawl back towards the factory. I'm a bit hesitant to follow her at first, but I figure she probably knows her way around better than I do, since she's been surviving out here for a while by herself.

She crawls along, staying in the dark jagged shadows next to the factory building. I stay close behind, ready to defend us if something was to happen. She continues to crawl through a little hole in the wall and I manage to squeeze my own body through. Then we find ourselves back in the dark factory once again.

Zoe stands up and stays hidden behind the boxes, dodging

loose pipes hanging from the ceiling. As she swerves her body from side to side, she's almost reached the other side of the room. She sure can move fast. I push myself up against the wall, following her. She obviously knows the hiding places around here pretty well. Her expression is filled with determination while she pulls a small knife out of her pocket. I automatically go to take it away from her, like I would do with…

Damn it, Ella! I will not allow myself to say her name. I cannot allow myself to picture her.

Suddenly, Zoe slices through a small rope in front of her as a large pipe falls from the ceiling, ready to crush anybody who walks past. A booby trap perhaps? Zoe turns around with a small, mischievous smile playing on her lips. My eyes are wide in shock but her cheeky grin makes me laugh. I've got to say, I'm quite impressed by this nine-year-old, and she really knows how to survive out here. I may learn a thing or two from her.

She starts to pull on a rope and a hidden staircase drops from above us. I then follow her up and we come to a small room in the top of the building. There is a cracked window right in the corner of the room. I can tell Zoe spends a lot of her time up here because there is a line of small cushions pushed up against the glass.

We must be at least forty feet high, and out the window I can see most of the streets below. Taking a seat on the cushions, we both look out to see where the gunfire has come from. The window in front of me, however, has got red markings drawn onto the stained glass. I stand back a little, trying to work out what they are. Zoe leads me back a little bit more and I start to see the window as a map of the town. An 'X' is marked on a few worn-down houses and a circle on others. I look down to find Zoe smirking.

"The X means I've got all the food in that house." She looks up at me, waiting for my reaction. Her little beaming smile shows how proud she is of what she's accomplished so far, and I can't help but smile at the clever, young girl standing next to me. She really is something. "The circles are houses I need to check out next." She bounces up and down and looks out the cracked glass again. "There!" She points and I walk back over.

The men march out of a house a few streets away, dragging a body behind them. It looks like a young boy about the same age as Zoe. I glance over at her but her face has fallen.

"Hey, it's okay." I put my hands on her shoulders and bring her around to face me. She nods hesitantly.

Why are they killing people? Aren't they supposed to be saving other survivors? My mind whirls in a hundred different directions, flitting from one idea to the next. I can't seem to come up with any answers that make sense, apart from one. We do need to get out of here before we make the top spot on their hit list.

"We should go now. There's a truck waiting for us at the edge of town." I hold Zoe's hand and pull her out of the building. We stay hidden in the shadows of the houses and start to head back to the truck. But another loud gunshot rumbles from nearby and we both freeze.

CHAPTER 13

LOOKING AROUND IN PANIC, KIRA and Dale come running towards us.

"Run!" Dale shouts, and we both start to sprint ahead. The dust and diseased carnage layers the old roads that surround us as we race on through the streets. A rotting smell explodes through the air, but we are quick so the odour doesn't linger for too long. Zoe's little legs move swiftly, running at the same pace as I am. Another loud gunshot goes off and we quickly take the next corner. Kira and Dale follow us and we all come to a stop in the nearby alleyway.

"Who's chasing you?" I ask, breathlessly. My knees shake with lack of stamina. Maybe we should've trained harder back at the Underground. Maybe Derrick was right — we're not ready to face the outside world. With something like lack of stamina, who knows how long we'll all survive out here.

"We don't know. Some guys randomly started shooting at us!"

Kira looks around, panicking and also out of breath. But unlike me, she gains her strength back in no time, leaving me holding my throbbing stitch that pierces my side.

"We need to get out of here!" Dale checks around the corner for any sign of them.

"We need to go that way." Zoe stands at my side and points to a little opening between the buildings next to us.

"Okay, you're new." Dale looks wide-eyed at Zoe's sudden appearance.

"No time." I say, as she pulls at my sleeve and we all squeeze through the little gap. Kira and Dale are hesitant to follow Zoe, but they don't have any other choice when the men sprint around the corner, looking for us.

"Wait, I forgot my sword. I'll be right back." I turn to run back towards the factory, but Dale grabs my arm.

"Ella, it's too late." His words pierce me straight through the heart. Those words, those exact words that haunt me every waking moment. The words that will forever be my living demon.

"It's never too late." I yank my arm away and run with everything in me.

As soon as I make it back to the factory door, I feel all my confidence shatter. *What have I done? I've left my friends because fear took over. My number one enemy has driven me to my worst nightmare.* I shake away my irrational thoughts and focus on getting my sword back. I'll be helpless without it.

The town has been quiet for a while. No one has followed me and I can't hear a single sound. I walk cautiously through the dim factory door, the wooden floorboards creaking underneath my boots. *Must find my sword.* I left it at the opening of Zoe's den. How could I be so careless?

Looking through each room, the small specks of light lead the way. My leg crashes against a few cardboard boxes and I curse out.

Stubbing my toes a few more times, I finally reach the den of boxes. Crawling through the tunnel, I grab my sword and turn to crawl back out. Suddenly I hear the floorboards creak behind me and I immediately freeze. The only sound is my ragged breathing. *Is someone in here with me? Did someone follow me? No, they couldn't. I'm just being paranoid.* Edging my way out again, I hear another creak. A louder one than the last.

The squelch of boots gets closer as I hold my sword close to my chest. The engraved letter 'E' shimmers in the light and I feel a strange sense of confidence — almost unnatural confidence that I instantly regret because I jump out of my hiding place and crash into a body.

"Not hiding, were we?" The yellow, revolting teeth snarl at me. As I step backwards, I trip over my own boots and land flat on the floor. My sword crashes against the ground and is now just out of reach.

Before me stands a six-foot man with deep, red eyes. His face is a mixture of excitement and curiosity. He wears all black and I see the yellow logo printed on his sleeve. *A soldier.*

"They march through and kill people." Zoe's words hit me like a brick and I carefully edge away from him.

"I'm not going to hurt you."

Yeah right. He hides a grin under the brown hair covering most of his chin. His eyebrows are dark, almost hauntingly dark, as if they carry their own secrets.

"Get away from me!" I say sternly, surprising myself. If I sound confident it's only because I'm terrified that I'm going to die. I can't die yet. There's too much I need to know, too many answers I seek, and I doubt Beardy over here is going to answer any of my questions.

"What fun would that be?" Suddenly he charges at me, snarling his teeth. He holds a dagger in his tight clasp and my eyes widen. I immediately kick him in the groin — a special move of mine — and he curses out.

"You little…" He's cut off when Dale runs at him and slams his own sword into the side of Beardy's head.

"Come on, Ella. Let's go!" He runs over and holds out his strong hand. In this one moment I see just how handsome Dale is. His jet black hair covers most of his face but the strands have parted slightly, revealing his hypnotic blue eyes.

"Ella!" he snaps, snapping me back to life.

I take his hand and pick up my sword, leaving Beardy lying on the ground. We run out the building, back towards the others.

"Ella, are you *crazy*? You're lucky you're still alive!" Kira shouts, pacing back and forth. She throws in some unrepeatable words and Zoe scowls at her.

"Look we don't…"

"Where are THEY?!" a booming voice echoes through the air. We all freeze, trying not to make a sound. I look down and find Zoe peering out into the streets.

"You LOST them, you idiot!" another voice booms.

Zoe pulls a gleaming knife out of her pocket and Kira looks at me with a confused and slightly alarmed expression. *That must have been how I looked when she first held a knife in front of me.* Zoe looks up and I see what's caught her eye. A few old dustbins sit on the opposite side of the road, and above them sits a small glass windowpane. Zoe narrows her eyes and effortlessly throws the knife through the air. I look around to see Dale's eyes popping out of his head as he witnesses a nine-year-old throwing a knife. The blade hits the window, smashing it into a million pieces. The shards of glass fall down and hit the dustbins. Suddenly a group of rats run, scattering out from underneath the bins.

"OVER THERE!" one of the men shout. They all run towards the dustbins, looking endlessly around for us.

"Come on." Zoe runs out and we all follow.

"Seriously, who is this little person?" Dale looks at me with eyebrows up to his hairline. I just laugh and run, taking Zoe's hand.

"There they go!" one of the men shouts from behind us, but we are long gone. The truck comes into view and Troy stands waiting at the side. He jumps up when he sees us all running towards him.

"What's wrong?" he shouts.

"Drive! Just drive!" I shout back and he climbs into the driver's seat. Kira and Dale hop in the back and I help Zoe up into the truck, then climb in after her.

I look out the back window while Troy starts up the engine to see the men run at us, aiming for our tires, but as the truck darts forward they get buried behind, with the dust from our quick departure.

"What the hell was that all about?" George and Jim look a little taken aback by our entrance.

"We were being chased," Zoe pipes up, sitting cross-legged on one of the leather seats. She tucks her school shoes under her bony knees before looking up innocently at George and Jim. They both look at her confused, probably wondering why a nine-year-old has popped up from nowhere.

"This is Zoe." I introduce her to George and Jim, who both introduce themselves. So do Kira and Dale, but Troy just continues to drive the truck, staying very quiet. I furrow my brows, wondering what he's thinking about.

"How's Mark?" I ask, looking at his body slumped up against the truck wall.

"Well, he hasn't improved but at least he's talking." George says, shrugging.

"What's wrong with him?"

"He's got an infected cut on his leg and his temperature has risen a lot in the last few hours," Jim says. Kira looks down sympathetically at Mark.

"He's asleep at the moment, but he needs some medicine," George says, sighing.

"And we're running out of fuel," Troy interrupts, from the front.

"You didn't find any?" I ask, raising my voice slightly so he can hear me from the back seat.

My arm is pressed against the back door and my back is squeezed into the tight corner. We've allowed just enough room for Mark to lay down, but each of us are shoulder to shoulder, trying to fight for more room.

"That's what I was going to tell you, but we had to leave in such a hurry." Troy gazes at me in the rearview mirror with those deep hazel eyes that hold too much emotion, and it makes my cheeks redden a little. "Another few miles and we'll be walking," he says, turning his attention back to driving.

Great. How's Mark going to walk anywhere? And how long can Zoe keep up with us if we do walk? I take a deep breath and lean my head against the seat.

"There's another town near here," Zoe speaks up, looking at our curious expressions.

"There is?" Kira raises an eyebrow.

"Yeah, a few miles away. I've never been there but it's supposed to be for rich, snobby people." Zoe giggles and goes back to playing with her torn plaid shorts.

Kira has a small smile layering on her face as she looks up at me. "That sounds tempting."

I laugh and shake my head. She's thinking the same thing I am.

"We're going to find this town and stop there. See if we can find any medicine or supplies," Kira speaks up.

"I'm going with you this time," Troy insists, gripping the steering wheel tightly.

"I'm coming too," I say, earning a glare from Troy.

"You're staying here," he grunts. All I want to do is laugh. He's trying to tell me what to do. *How sweet.*

"I'm coming," I repeat more firmly. Troy mumbles something under his breath.

"You two stay and look after Mark," Kira says, looking at George and Jim.

"But we could…"

"Someone needs to stay with him," Dale says. He looks up out of his dark eyes. His shaggy black hair falls in front of his face, hiding the dark rings outlining the vivid, electric blue.

"Me, Ella, and Troy will go," Dale states. He stands up and climbs into the front seat next to Troy. Probably to help find this town of Zoe's.

"Can I come?" Zoe pleads with me, moving closer to my side.

She's still very wary of the others and looks slightly overwhelmed by the amount of people here. I guess that's only fair because she's been living and surviving on her own for a while now. I don't like the idea of letting her come along, just in case we come face to face with the very thing we are running from. I don't like the idea of letting anyone come along, full stop. Not since what happened with Terry. Sighing, I think it over. I guess I can't go on my own and we need all the food and supplies we can get. I look down at Zoe's big brown eyes and laugh at her pleading expression.

"Okay, but we stay together." I ruffle her long, red hair and she laughs.

"Okay."

We look out the truck windows for what seems like hours, and we still haven't found any sign of a single town. Mark only seems to be getting worse. His shivering body is hunched up in one of the backseats. Kira has her arm wrapped tightly around his shoulder, trying to comfort him the best she can. I can see the worry in her eyes as his body quivers in pain. George and Jim sit next to Dale equally as worried. I block out all the noise and clear my mind. We need to head north to The Society. To get there we need more supplies, especially if we are going to be on foot soon. Zoe leans her head on me and her eyes start to close. I smile and let her drift off for a while. The more sleep she gets, the better — especially if we have to fight those monsters again.

I open my eyes to the truck shaking from side to side. I must have fallen asleep. Zoe still leans her head on me and Kira lays her head against Mark. The truck bumps over the rocky ground beneath us and I rub my eyelids.

"I think we've found it," Troy announces, from the front. I turn to look out the window, trying not to disturb Zoe, and see a dark shadows in the distance. Squinting my eyes I can make out the haunting silhouettes of tall buildings and grand houses. As we get closer, the truck comes to a stop and the engine shuts off.

"Well, that's all the fuel gone." Troy turns around in his seat and faces me. "Ready?" He raises an eyebrow and I nod.

I slide Zoe off me and walk out the back of the truck. Dale joins us at the side and I hold the handle of my sword, ready to defend myself if necessary. If I leave Zoe here, she might get some more sleep and the others are here to protect her if something was to go wrong. Her body needs the rest and so does Kira's. George and Jim nod at me as the three of us leave. They sit next to Zoe, keeping an eye out for any danger. We start to walk towards the silhouettes in the distance. My boots are covered in dirt and dust from the dry ground around us. The hard surface is easy enough to walk on, although my feet are starting to get raging blisters. I shake away the small, stinging pains and focus on what's in front of us. Dale walks ahead, swinging his gleaming sword around to keep himself occupied. I roll my eyes.

After a while, the silhouettes suddenly start to come into view. I look back at the truck but it's now out of sight. We must have walked about two miles by now.

"You should've stayed." Troy walks next to me. His face is blank as he looks ahead of us, staying alert for danger.

"What do you mean, I should've stayed?" *How dare he tell me what I should and shouldn't do?*

"You can't take responsibility for everything." He looks at me.

"I don't," I snap back.

"You do. We all decided to leave together, and it's not your fault we're all out here." He looks into my eyes and I look away.

"It is. We should've never left. Terry might still be alive if we hadn't..."

"He might be dead either way. We all could have been, if we stayed," Troy sighs, his expression searching mine — searching me for any sign of guilt, frustration, or uneasiness. It's like being on a journey with a futuristic robot that scans you every five minutes. I can't tell whether I like the fact that he cares so much about what I'm feeling, or curious as to why he's so interested.

"Ella, you don't need to worry about all of us, we're a team. We work together."

"I know. I just want to protect everyone. I can't let anyone else get hurt." I shake my head and wipe away one glistening tear off my cheek. I don't know whether it's from the scorching pain of my blisters or the pure agony of losing Terry.

"I know you do," he replies, curtly.

"Why do you care what I feel?" I ask, immediately wanting to take the words back. But it's too late.

His head whips around to face me. His hazel eyes staring at me. Almost glaring. "Why wouldn't I care?" He cocks his head to the side. *Why do I feel like he's scanning me yet again?*

"You just seem so interested in what I'm feeling all the time." I can't wriggle out of this one now, so I may as well dig deeper and find out what his problem is. He doesn't reply but looks straight ahead, running his fingers through that gorgeous short hair of his. *Wait, did I just say that?* "I mean, it's not like we've known each other for very long and you seem more interested in what I'm feeling than worrying about zombies attacking. I mean…"

"Whoa, Ella. Slow down." He looks at me, a little amused, and then takes a deep breath. "I like to know that you're okay."

"Why?" I crease my brows.

"We're a team, aren't we?"

I nod. We both walk together in silence after our little conversation, watching Dale sling his sword around a few yards ahead.

"You're not what I'm used to." Troy's expression hardens, and I can't keep quiet long enough to soak in the strong contours of his face, the light stubble on his jaw.

"I'm not what you're used to?" My voice comes out a lot squeakier than I originally would have liked.

"You're different. You're…"

"Soooo, what are we talking about?" A small singsong voice comes from my side. I look down and find Zoe walking in between us. I laugh but Troy doesn't look impressed. "I wasn't going to stay behind and miss everything." She walks off just ahead of me, keeping close. I guess you can't leave a mischievous nine-year-old behind and expect her to stay put.

Finally, after another few miles, we can start to see the houses clearly. Some have white, broken fences with rotting plants in the gardens, and others are merely burnt to the ground with nothing to show for them but dust.

"Here we are." Troy dusts off a sign with his hand.

Ringwood

I guess this is it. The sign is smothered in dirt and a few bloodied handprints. Zoe's eyes widen but it doesn't faze her and she keeps walking forward. We follow her through the abandoned streets. The lonely, empty houses stand tall around us. Each window is smashed and the front doors are broken, most probably from a zombie attack. The beautiful wooden porches and bright green gardens, surrounded by gleaming white fences, are no longer. The grass is replaced by brown rotting weeds and the mouldy fences are half missing. The half that is still there has either fallen over, or is leaning over to one side.

Zoe walks ahead of us and starts to explore. This town is silent, too silent.

CHAPTER 14

I KEEP AWARE FOR DANGER as we continue to walk, kicking large rocks and grey stones off the cracked road.

"Right, we need as much food and medicine as we can find, before it gets dark," Dale says. He stops in front and turns toward us.

"Okay, I'll take that house," I say, pointing to a house with a half burnt roof and black walls.

"Okay, split up and shout if something's wrong. Stay close." Dale runs off into another house.

Troy looks hesitant to leave me and Zoe standing there. But a thought registers through his mind and he nods at me, walking off towards a building on his left — carrying his confidence and bravery with him. Somehow knowing that he's around makes me feel slightly at ease. Knowing that we're a team makes me feel part of a family again.

"Come on," I say to Zoe, watching Troy walk away, my eyes

lingering on him for slightly longer than necessary. As I turn back around, Zoe wiggles her eyebrows up and down. I laugh.

"You like him." She giggles.

"Do not," I reply. Too quickly, I might add.

"You're getting defensive." She scowls with a mischievous smirk on her face.

"I don't like him, like that."

"Like what?" She grins. I sigh, realising she's really not going to let this go.

"I don't like him, Zoe." I sound firm and in control. *Does my voice deceive me?*

"Whatever you say." She skips off towards the house and I follow behind, grinning at her constant happiness within this nightmare of a world.

"This place is quiet," Zoe whispers, looking around and narrowing her eyes.

"Yeah, I thought that." We both stay aware as we walk up the once white, magical porch.

We step over rotting ligaments left behind on the bloodstained steps, and carefully hoist ourselves over the missing pieces of wooden floor. When we finally reach the doorway, the front door squeaks open, echoing through the silent hallway in front of us. By the way the door hangs on its hinges, it looks as if someone forced their way in. Also judging by the bloodstained walls, the family is no longer living here. We are careful not to tread on any of the broken glass on the floor since the more noise we make we could attract more zombies. Zoe tiptoes around, looking at the crooked family pictures. Each one hangs diagonally on the flowery wallpaper.

"They look really happy." Zoe tilts her head to the side, studying the family's happy smiles and picks the photo off the wall. As she lifts it off the metal nail, the back is covered in green slime and she drops it to the floor in shock.

"Eww!" She shivers and steps away from it. I scrunch my nose up at the smell seeping from the gross slime.

"What is that?" I ask, walking over to it.

"I don't know." Zoe looks up at me, covering her own nose.

"It looks new. It would've decomposed by now if it was old," I say, looking around warily.

The house is still silent as we walk around. Every step we take just seems to make us more nervous. Eventually we find the kitchen and raid the cupboards to find packets and tins of food everywhere. Filling our backpacks, we are set for the next few days. Zoe opens a packet of stale biscuits from the cupboard, offering me one, and begins to munch away. I decline the offer, since she needs all the food she can get and I need to keep her energy up. The packet is gone within a few minutes, so we make our way upstairs to see if we can find anything else. The floorboards creak as we walk up the stairs to the upper level of the house. We are met with another dark hallway and lots more pictures hanging proudly on the wall. The only window is at the end of the hall as the moonlight shines onto the floor, highlighting footsteps covered in green slime. I crease my brows at the sight.

Suddenly, Zoe steps onto a floorboard and it breaks underneath her foot. She screams when her leg gets caught, dangling from the ceiling. I run to help her but before I can get there, a zombie runs for me. Its teeth drool with hunger and want while its body shakes with starvation. Zoe screams and I immediately take my defensive position. Grabbing my sword, I hold my ground and raise the gleaming tip into the air. Zoe's eyes are filled with horror as she watches me slice through the monster's head, and it rolls across the floor. When I look up, I see four more zombies lunging for me. *Where are they coming from?*

Zoe can't move and tries her best to force her leg out of the floorboards, but she doesn't have enough strength. I don't have the time to help her because two of the zombies start to cage us in. I stand in front of Zoe and protect her the best I can from the monsters that murdered her parents. This is exactly what I wanted to avoid. I punch the second zombie in the face and it staggers backward, hitting its jagged spine against the wall. I curse under my breath from the agony of my now raw knuckles. The zombie gets back on its feet, but before it has a chance, Zoe throws one of her knives, stabbing it straight through the heart. With my other hand, I slice the arm off the fourth zombie and it cries out in agony. The other two zombies try to grab at my clothes, my hair, and anything else they can grip onto, but I swing my arm around, destroying limbs. But I eventually slip in the pile of green goo, hitting my head on the floor, and I curse out. A grotesque hand grabs my hair and I feel myself being yanked backwards. I hear a growl next to my neck and the warm breath on my skin. Panicking, I immediately ram my elbow into the monster's head. It yelps in surprise when I stab it in the gut. Howling and screaming fill the air as a zombie runs for Zoe. Her forehead is covered with sweat and she struggles to break free from the floorboards, but she can't move. I feel the confidence build and the fear leave me as I dive over her body and slice through the last remaining zombie.

Breathing silently, I look at the dead bodies surrounding us. Six zombies in total. Six deaths. Using the last of my strength, I lift Zoe out and she sits there holding her leg in pain.

"Zoe, what's hurting?" I ask.

"Just my leg. That's all. It's fine." She gets up and limps next to me.

"You're not fine, Zoe." I try to help her walk but she winces when she steps on her foot. I pick her up and decide to find Troy and Dale. We've got enough food so maybe they've found some medicine elsewhere. As I walk down the stairs, a strange noise comes from across the room. I look up to see another deadly zombie blocking the doorway. Its eyes are distant and hungry. It starts to run at me. *Not another one*. I hold Zoe in my arms, not knowing what to do.

"Ella!" Zoe screams, and hides into my jacket. Her body shakes with fear and in that one moment, she reminds me of Leila. Her terrified expression reminds me of how scared she was. How she was so brave and fought against her emotions to let me go.

I look up at the beast running at me. Anger and fury burn throughout me as I run left, dodging the zombie. Its confused expression momentarily slows it down enough for me to place Zoe down and grab broken plank of wood off the floor. It runs at me again, moving fast as I effortlessly break the flimsy bit of wood in two. My eyes widen at its pace — it's running faster than I anticipated. It's about five feet away when I sprint towards it. The zombie lunges for me and using the adrenaline coursing through me, I jump and land on its back. As it tries to throw me off, I cling on for dear life. It finally stops moving and before it has time to attack Zoe, who is just left huddled up on the floor, I take the broken piece of wood and pierce it through the zombie's back. It lets out a howl of pain while its body crumbles to the floor. The wood sticks out of the creature's back and I let out an inhale of breath. I stare at the disgusting creature and kick it as I walk towards Zoe.

"Come on, before we run into any more," I say, picking her up. She nods quickly and I carry her out of the doorway. Troy and Dale are running over to the house and stop immediately when they see us.

"What happened?" Dale looks out of breath, his eyes darting between me and Zoe.

"A zombie." I answer, walking over to them. "Zoe's hurt her leg." I hold her tight in my arms.

Dale takes her off me and lets her climb safely onto his back.

"Did you find anything?" I ask.

"Just a load of junk," Troy speaks up. He looks distracted. I crease my brows trying to figure out what's got his attention.

"Where to now?" Dale asks.

"Shh," Troy ignores Dale's question, holding up his hand and looking around warily. "Something's not right." He takes out his sword as the silent wind whistles past us.

The breeze whisks past my blonde hair as Zoe shivers. The revolting smell travels with the wind, filling my senses.

"We have to get out of here." Troy starts to walk off and we all follow, staying alert. We trudge to the end of the street in silence with Dale carrying Zoe on his back. Me and Troy walk alongside them, our feet thudding together against the ground. The foggy air blocks the view ahead, but soon enough something comes into view. Figures are moving towards us, a group of figures. Different shapes and sizes stalk in our direction. I squint my eyes and stop dead in my tracks. Dale and Troy do the same. The figures start to run, dark eyes gleaming in the fog. Soon enough a whole group of zombies are sprinting for us. I no longer feel the fear and the horror my family felt. The horror that scared me into hiding underground. There is only one thing to do now.

Immediately I grab my sword out of its case, standing my ground. Troy looks over to me and nods. He's ready to fight. I can only smile at his determination. I nod back as we begin defences. Dale runs behind, trying to keep Zoe safe. The group of zombies are getting faster, now running at an almighty speed. The smell of fresh meat must be drawing them close to us. Their drooling, open mouths and the jagged, rotting teeth come into view as the horrific smell surrounds us. The first zombie runs at me and I slice off its head in one quick swipe. Turning around, I stab another straight through the heart. They both roar in agony when they fall to the floor, eventually bleeding out — the diseased toxin leaving their rotting veins, dry corpses that will soon turn to ash. Suddenly, little droplets of rain start to fall from the weeping sky above us. Small, glistening tears soon become a harder, thunder of rain. The hail thuds to the ground, covering and drenching us all. The ground has become a river of mud underneath our feet, making the ground slippery and harder to keep upright.

It does work to our advantage though because it slows down the monsters aiming for us.

They run from every direction. More and more. We hear their thundering footsteps in the deep puddles and immediately know what direction they're coming from. I twirl around and smash my sword against the broken skull of a monster behind me, before twirling around again to stab another one. Howls of pain fill the air as Troy fights off the zombies surrounding him. His muscular arms move slowly, cutting through the diseased skin of the beasts. He shouts out and stabs another. The rain drenches his clothes and his strong frame of muscles is hard to ignore as his wet T-shirt sticks against the raw strength he unleashes.

I shout out when one grabs my leg. Its body drags itself along the floor as its other arm clasps my ankle. I scream, realising its head is rolling on the floor two feet away. *How can it still be alive?* I immediately cut off its hands and step out of its clasp. I stamp on its back causing its narrow bones to crack underneath my feet, stabbing my sword through its back for good measure. I'm lucky it had no teeth to bite me or I would've been dead.

A few more run at me and I dodge them, running towards Troy. He kills the last one surrounding him and watches me run over. He's immediately drawn to the torn slashes on my trousers where the zombie had grabbed me and his eyes turn dark, almost murderous. He quickly examines me for any other injuries and I narrow my eyes with determination. Dale stands off to the side in a safer location, fighting off the few around him, protecting Zoe. She has hidden behind an old tire on the ground and peers out at the war-zone in front of her. Her terrified little eyes scan the scene as she holds out her small knife, just in case.

"Ella, duck!" Troy yells at me. I drop to the floor just in time as a zombie falls over the top of me. It lands on the ground and Troy slices it in half, green blood oozing out of its insides. I look up at him wide eyed. He then grabs my hand, wasting no time, and takes me over to Dale. We help fight off the last few and I leave Dale and Troy to fight off the last one as I run over to Zoe, but she's gone. I hastily scan the area for her. No sign.

"Zoe!" I scream. Dale and Troy both look around at me. It doesn't take them long to figure out what's wrong.

We all rummage around, searching the area.

"Zoe?!" I shout out.

I hear a scream coming from within the fog ahead and run towards the tortured sound. I hold out my gleaming sword, the tip covered in green zombie blood, evidence of murder. Another scream and I see her. She holds out her arms in front of her as a zombie leans over her body. She hides under a wooden crate while the monster desperately smashes it apart in an effort to reach her.

"Help!" she screams, the crate slowly starting to crush her. I sprint over to them. She screams again as the crate digs into her skin, slowly squashing her to death.

I hold my sword to the air and take off the zombie's legs, causing its torso to crumble to the floor. Its body collapses on top of the crate and I grab Zoe, pulling her out before it completely gives way. I stare at the beast and pull Zoe close, holding her face in my hands to check if she's okay.

"What happened?" Dale runs over. Blood covers him from head-to-toe and dark circles lay underneath his eyes. Troy checks us both over. He equally looks as tired.

"Thank you." Zoe looks up and hugs me, causing me to smile. I welcome her affection and am just glad she's alright. Her body starts to relax — we all do, putting away our weapons.

"Zombies are everywhere here." Dale looks at me in concern. He points back to the way we came. Through the midst of the fog, I can see movement — dark silhouettes stalking every inch of life, searching for us. There is no way we can head back. It's a death trap.

"We will have to carry on this way. It's not safe back there." Troy helps Zoe up onto his back, where she feels safe. I'd feel safe there too, if I was small enough for him to carry. *Wow. Okay, I'm more tired than I thought.*

"But what about the others?" I ask, horrified at what Troy's implying.

"It might be too late for them." He looks at the floor, his expression giving nothing away. "Those monsters are flooding the place. We have to keep moving." He sighs.

"We have to go back and check if they need help!" I start to walk back, but Troy grabs my arm.

"It's a suicide mission, Ella!" His face tells me he's serious, the bleeding determination filling the deep hazel of his eyes. For a moment I feel like fleeing, punching and kicking my way back to the others, but then I think of Zoe. She has to be safe. Even if it means leaving them.

"I-I can't," I stutter, my eyes darting from Troy to the fog.

"You must. I've seen your strength and your equally powerful stubbornness, but this time I'm not backing down. No matter how much you argue, I can't let you do this. I will not risk your life, even if it means dragging you by your hair. Trust me, I can play rough." His eyes darken even more. *Was that a threat?*

Even if I was planning to run, to escape his shield, I would need a much stronger force. His hard expression means business and I'm in no position to argue. But it won't stop me. I tug at his arm once again, trying to break free. Something in me just needs to save them, to warn them what's out here. *I need to do something!*

"I mean it. If you want this the hard way, I have no problem carrying you."

How humiliating.

"You'll get killed. We need to carry on. They might make it." Dale interrupts the raging emotion between us, the bull and the lion fighting to the death. Eventually one must give in and it's not going to be me.

"I. Can't. Leave. Them." I think about Kira and Mark. His injury. George and Jim. The group we've left behind. *No!*

I don't have time to think as Troy places Zoe down on the ground and grabs my waist, tossing me over his shoulder.

"Hey!" I shout, but he ignores me.

"You're the biggest pain I've ever met, Ella," Troy mumbles. No matter how much I kick and squirm, it doesn't affect him in the slightest. He just continues to carry me, taking my sword and handing it to Dale to be on the safe side. *As if I'd threaten him with my weapon to escape. Pfft.*

Dale follows behind Troy, carrying Zoe. After a few miles, I finally give up. He's taken my dignity and my sword. I'll just have to play it his way this once. Zoe looks up at me with an *I feel sorry for you* expression. I sigh, unable to help but wonder whether all of our friends will survive.

Finally Troy has put me down and as we walk further away, the groans from the zombies start to fade out, the eerie silence filling the air once again. The rain has stopped hammering down and it's only a light shower now. We continue to walk for miles, making sure to put enough distance between us and the zombies as possible. The pain of leaving the others behind stabs me in the gut with every step that we walk further away from them. The longer we walk, the guiltier I feel. We could have done something, warned them even. But that means putting Zoe in danger and I realise now that she could've got very hurt. Dale and Troy both take turns to carry Zoe since her leg is still too painful for her to walk on.

The moon still looms over us, following us wherever we go. Finally, we decide to stop and campout for the night. We find an old tree bark, standing on its own in the middle of nowhere. Dale reaches into his bag and pulls out a reel of string. He ties it to the bark and one end to the floor. Taking off his shirt, he squeezes out the river of water. He places it on the thin line of string. I put the bags down on the floor and get out the small blanket from within my backpack. I hand it to Zoe and she thanks me, laying her head against the backpacks for a pillow. We decide not to make a fire because it might attract more zombies. I suddenly look up to find a shirtless Dale walking towards me, his physique ripped with muscles and a slight tan. His hair is still damp from the rain and the moonlight highlights every hill and curve bulging on his upper arms while he takes off his boots and gently sits next to me. His feet are covered in blisters and mine aren't much better.

"How're you holding up?" He looks at me from under his dark, dishevelled hair.

"I'm okay." I smile weakly.

"Ella, we had to leave them behind. There was nothing you could've done." He looks apologetic.

"I know. I keep thinking that this is just one horrible nightmare that I'm going to wake up from." I shake my head at the thought. Dale smiles sympathetically and looks up into the sky. Twinkling stars fill the darkness and glisten, gleaming down on us.

"I won't let anything happen to you." Dale still gazes into the sky and I watch him carefully. I study his clenched jaw, and the way he holds hope and adoration for the stars gleaming within his eyes. "I won't let anything happen to any of you." He looks back around at me, and then at Zoe, who is fast asleep and wrapped up in a blanket.

Troy walks over and gently lifts her up, carrying her over to where we're sitting. Troy gives me and Dale a strange look before placing Zoe on the nearest blanket. The closer we are together, the safer we'll be. Her face looks peaceful as she escapes this horrible world, entering the wonderland of her dreams.

"I'm sorry, Ella," Troy says. He sits opposite us on the ground, pulling out an extra jumper since it's starting to get chilly. "I'm sorry we had to leave them. I know they were your friends." He looks over at me and hands me the jumper. "Here, take this."

"I've already got a jacket. It's fine," I say, brushing him off. He's only got a soaking wet shirt on, so he should wear it.

"Ella, just take it." He holds it out to me with the same hard expression he usually wears.

"Thank you." I smile and pull it over my head.

"You should get some sleep. I'll take the first watch." Troy watches me.

"I can take the first watch. You look tired, and I don't need that much sleep anyway." I start to stand, but Troy beats me to it.

"Get some sleep, Ella. I mean it," he demands. Troy walks over to a rock, taking a seat. He looks out, keeping watch, holding his gun next to his chest.

I guess I should sleep whilst I have the chance. I'm too tired to argue with him. I look around to see Dale has made himself as comfortable as he can on the dusty ground. He lays on his jacket and I do the same. I clutch the warm jumper tighter around me while I lean my head against one of the backpacks. The warm material smells of Troy and I can't help but smile as I lay on my back, looking up at the night sky. It's the most beautiful thing I've seen for a while. I eventually feel my eyelids close, drifting off into my own world of demons.

CHAPTER 15

I WAKE SUDDENLY, BOLTING UPRIGHT with sweat dripping off my forehead, my breathing erratic as I try to slow my heartbeat down. Another nightmare. I look around to find Dale and Zoe peacefully sleeping on the ground. Troy still sits on the large rock, watching out for any danger. The distant call of grasshoppers and the forest of trees standing only a few miles away remind me of the small amount of life, still battling on. I get up and wrap my jacket tightly around me. Pulling the material close, I instantly warm up from the cold night. I cautiously walk over to where Troy sits and he looks up slowly when he sees my approach.

"How long was I asleep?" I ask, taking a seat next to him, holding the jumper he gave me against my erratically beating heart. *Why am I so nervous around him?*

The cold rock is hard and quite uncomfortable to sit on but it's nothing compared to the harsh chill of the night. A slight sting of ice wraps its way over my skin as soon as I sit down.

"A few hours." He looks off into the distance.

"Right," I mumble. "Can I ask you something?"

"Sure." He looks around to face me, wearing a soft smile. *Whoa, change of personality*. The soft side of Troy. I can work with that.

"How did you end up in the Underground?"

He takes a deep breath. "My town was attacked. My family didn't make it. I had to leave them behind. Me and a few others made it to the truck in time," he sighs. "I keep thinking back. I keep replaying it in my head. I might have been able to save them if..." He stops and shakes his head, throwing a large stone out into the darkness.

"If what?"

"I don't know," he replies.

"You can't think back. You just, can't." My voice breaks with my own memories as I look out into the distance. I can feel the heat from his gaze rising by the second.

"You're different, Ella." He massages the back of his neck, as if the words are hard for him to say. I just stare at him.

He lets out a sigh, holding his head in his hands. The strong veins and muscular arms flex in the moonlight. I wonder what it would feel like, to have those arms wrapped around me. To feel the raw touch of our skin, the heat of his body against mine. I widen my eyes and stop my irrational thinking.

"You argue with me. No one has ever argued with me like that," he says slowly.

"Everyone just bows to you? Like you're their king?" I say, with slight sarcasm.

His lips twitch into a small, amused smile as he looks round at me.

"For some reason, I find your stubborn attitude quite charming." He grins. *Another personality change*. I must admit, I do like this playful side to him.

"I'm going to catch a few hours sleep and you should too. You'll need your energy." Troy turns serious and looks up as Dale walks over to us.

"I'll keep watch. You two get some rest," Dale interrupts, looking between me and Troy with a strange expression. Troy helps me to my feet as Dale takes a seat on the rock.

"I've had enough sleep, I can…"

"Ella get some rest. You haven't had enough." Troy takes one more look at me and then at Dale, before walking over to where Zoe lays fast asleep. I follow behind him, looking back at Dale — who is watching out into the night — as we lay our heads down, one on each side of Zoe.

I can't sleep. I can't rest knowing that we might not make it. The thought of losing any more friends slices through my chest. I try not to think back, back to my family and Leila. Back to how Henry sacrificed himself for us. He didn't have to do that if we were prepared. Why didn't anyone warn us? I think back to what Derrick said. My parents are part of The Society. Why didn't they do anything? They could've saved Leila and Henry from this. They didn't have to get murdered like that. We didn't have to lose Terry either. No one deserves to die like that. A million questions invade my mind but I eventually start to drift off to sleep, carrying the loss and emptiness I feel inside.

I wake up to the delightful smell of food cooking. I rub my eyes and look around. Squinting in the in the morning daylight I find Dale, Troy, and Zoe sitting round a small fire. I immediately get up and walk over.

"Won't the fire attract more zombies?" I ask, panicked.

"Good morning to you too, cupcake." Dale winks at me.

"We need to eat and we can put it out when the food is cooked. I don't think there's a zombie around for miles," Troy replies, cooking the food over the roaring fire as Zoe beams up at me. She can't sit still at the thought of eating proper food. I laugh and sit down, still yawning from the lack of sleep. Dale and Zoe sit together, talking. I'm glad Zoe has gotten used to him — it's nice for her to be around people again.

"Here." Troy hands me bark of wood filled with a steaming plate of food. I don't ask what it is. I don't think I want to know.

"Thanks." I smile and dig in. Zoe and Dale do the same. As soon as this morning's food is gone, we put out the fire and pack up our belongings.

"Where are we going?" Zoe asks. I look down at her pale leg, which has a small bandage wrapped around her swollen knee.

"Don't worry, Ella. It's a mild strain. Zoe's leg will be back to normal in a few days. We will carry her most of the time, but the injury will heal quicker if you begin to move the joint as soon as you are able to do so, without experiencing significant pain that is." Dale raises his eyebrows.

"Are you a doctor or something?" I ask, almost in awe.

"Long story," Dale mumbles.

"We're headed north." Troy sits down, answering Zoe's earlier question and shows her the map Derrick gave us. "If the others are smart enough to follow the original plan, then they may catch up to us." *I seriously hope so.*

I can't help but feel a stab of guilt again. I know Dale feels the same way, because he shuffles closer and carefully places a strong arm over my shoulders in an effort to comfort me.

"I think we're about here. A few miles east of Ringwood." Troy points to a spot on the map and we all nod. As he looks up, his eyes are immediately drawn to Dale's arm around my shoulders.

He doesn't say anything but I can see his eyes darken a little.

"But why are we going that way?" Zoe looks confused, dragging Troy's attention back to her.

"We're going to The Society," I speak up, interrupting the two, but Zoe still looks at me with a blank expression.

"We think they're our best chance of survival. They may know more than what they're letting on about the zombie attacks. They may have found a cure," I say.

Zoe nods, finally understanding and starts to pack up her things. She has already neatly folded the blanket and given it back to me. I don't mention the fact that my parents might still be alive to the others, but then I remember that I let it slip to Zoe. Hopefully she can keep a secret. My sister and brother may be alive as well if my parents had survived it, but the chances are rather thin. I need to stay focused on surviving now. I need to keep us all alive.

Once we have packed up absolutely everything, we start to head north. "We should get to a town at least by dark, somewhere to camp out for the night." Troy leads us along.

Zoe rides on Dales back. She sighs, upset that she can't walk by herself. We walk over the dusty ground as the small rocks hit the bottom of my boots, causing me to wince. The raging blisters on my feet send bolts of pain up my leg, but I carry on. I won't be stopping for just a few blisters.

"Ella, are you alright?" Dale walks alongside me, carrying a bored-looking Zoe.

"Yeah, just a few blisters that's all," I say, looking at him. He has his shirt back on and his short black hair has dried from the shower of rain yesterday. He looks somewhat different, more grown-up perhaps? Maybe it's the thin layer of dark stubble growing across his jaw line.

"I know how you feel." Dale winces as the rocks hit his own boots.

Troy suddenly stops and we all look around to see why. A lone truck sits just ahead of us.

The dark Land Rover is on its side and covered in masses of blood.

“Is that?” I shout, running over to it.

“Ella!” Troy runs after me.

I stop and look at it. It’s got to be our truck. It looks exactly the same.

“Ella, stop. You don’t know what’s in it.” Troy catches up to me and holds me back, the heat from his hand lapping over my upper arms. He looks at the truck as Dale walks around the vehicle, examining it.

“Yep, this is ours,” he says, nodding. *What the hell happened? Where’s Kira and Mark? Where’s George and Jim?*

Zoe hides her head in Dale’s shoulder as I walk over to the overturned truck and try to pull open the driver door. It swings open and snaps off, scaring me a little. The smell quickly explodes out of the passenger seats and I pull back, resisting the odour. I can’t see much inside. I stand back from the smell, covering my nose with my hand, turning around to face the others. They all hold their noses as well.

“Ugh!” Zoe has disgust written all over her face.

“Ella, watch out!” Troy runs at me and I turn around just in time to see a body climb out of the truck. Not a human body. An undead, diseased body. Its eyes are dark and it still has patches of mangled hair. I immediately recognise Jim hiding underneath the virus that’s spread throughout his body.

“Jim?” My mouth gapes open.

He has venom and hunger in his eyes — clearly Jim is no longer with us. I feel a chorus of pain, knowing another of my friends has succumb to the deadly virus. The monster climbs out of the truck door and is just about to lunge for me, but a loud gunshot goes off and it hits him straight in the forehead. He falls backward and lands on the floor, spluttering out green blood. My eyes are wide, watching him. Troy puts down his gun and Dale runs over with Zoe, putting a steady arm on my shoulder.

"Jim didn't deserve that," I say, looking at his rotting body.

"He wasn't in there anymore, Ella." Troy looks at him.

"I know, but he didn't deserve to die. No one does." I put my hands to my head, trying to deal with everything. It's starting to get to me. We are losing more people every day. When is it going to stop? When we're *all* dead? I close my eyes and mourn over Jim's body. He willingly left the Underground with us, and this is what happens?

"The others aren't here." Troy looks inside the truck and the driver door too. "They could've got away." The hope in his eyes stings my heart a little.

I hope they're safe. I know Kira wouldn't give up without a fight. Mark wouldn't let anything happen to her, but with his bad leg who knows what happened. A little hand takes mine and Zoe looks at me with a sympathetic smile on her face. I smile back and remind myself of what's important right now. I need to survive. We need to survive. I won't let anything happen to any more of us, if I can help it.

We walk on, leaving the truck miles back, the air becoming hotter as the sun beats down on us. Sweat forms around my hairline while we trek towards the next town before dark. On the map it says it's about twenty miles north of Ringwood. We haven't had a break yet. My feet throb with every step, my blisters becoming worse, and the heat doesn't help. It only slows us down. We each take a gulp of the only bottle of water we have left and finally see something coming up ahead. I can make out the edge of a road buried under the rubble around us. The surface is easier to walk on and it leads us ahead. The sun starts to go in after a few more miles and the air has started to get cooler. Dale places Zoe on the ground to see if she can walk on her leg and she starts to hobble on her feet, wincing with every step, but at least she's trying. Dale picks her up again, like the gentleman he is, and Troy walks just ahead of me, keeping his eyes open for danger.

"Do you think there are any more zombies here?" Zoe whispers to me.

"I don't know, but I really hope not," I reply.

CHAPTER 16

WE FINALLY MAKE IT TO the town in front of us. Staying alert for any zombies we walk along the dusty road. The town is silent, and I can't see any sign of life whatsoever. We wander around for a while and find a grand, brick building in the middle of the street. The cracked windows are tinted black with smoke but the front door still looks intact. The silver number reads forty-two with red roses and small lilies painted perfectly over the frame. The wooden porch has a few broken floorboards but a wonderful, wooden bench sits in the corner, looking out into the street. The other houses that sit neatly apart from one another are not so grand, so we finally choose this one and head for the front door.

Troy and I walk on through, leaving Dale outside with Zoe. We walk around the dark hallways, checking for any zombies or dead bodies, but we see nothing and give Dale the all-clear. After sorting out our backpacks, we all sit around in the front room. The pale, pink sofas are ripped and torn. A stale, stuffy smell still lingers throughout the house. The building has two floors with a metal, spiral staircase leading to the upstairs hallway. Two bedrooms sit opposite one another along the hallway, with a small bathroom down the end. Downstairs, there is a marvellous gleaming kitchen and the living room, where we now sit. Night has fallen outside and the moonlight glistens through the shadowed windows.

Surprisingly, all the glass windows are still intact and the wooden floor is in great condition. We haven't found any food in the kitchen, except for a horrible smell coming from the fridge, but there's no way I'm opening a fridge door *ever* again, especially after last time. So instead, we open up a can of food from within our backpacks and share it between us, munching it down.

"It should be safe here for a while," Troy says. He paces up and down the room, regarding the outside world from window to window.

"Yeah, I haven't seen or heard any zombies for a while," Dale joins in. I nod but still feel wary.

This house seems too good to be true. Things seem too good to be true. Things are never this easy. Why now? Why have we found this spectacular house without any faults? Things just don't add up. Is this the calm before the storm? *Maybe*. I shake my head in defeat.

"Ella, you can relax a little." Dale cocks his head to the side.

"I know, I'm going to lay down." I walk up the stairs, leaving Dale, Troy, and Zoe sitting on the sofas. I need some rest, I need a place to think rationally, and I need to clear my head while I still can.

I lay my head down on the double bed in one of the two bedrooms. We've decided that I will stay in one room with Zoe. Dale and Troy will share the other room, taking it in turns to sleep on the bed and floor. I close my eyes but can't seem to drift off. All the madness from the last few days seems to be haunting me, and the fact that there is nothing I can do is killing me. I can't seem to help save everyone and the thought breaks my heart. My friends are dying. They're dying because I can't protect them. I can't do a thing about it. Innocent lives are being lost. I need to keep the people I'm with now safe. I cannot afford to think like this — I need to stay strong and hold back any feelings I have. Any emotion I feel needs to be pushed away because I need to focus on staying alive. A knock at the door startles me and I twist around to see Troy standing in the doorway.

"Ella, you awake?" He looks at me.

"Yeah, come in," I reply, sitting up and wrapping myself in the warm blankets. The soft cotton caresses my aching body. This is the most comfort I've felt in a long while and the feeling is exquisite.

"You okay?" He asks the question carefully, watching me as he takes a seat on the bed.

I shuffle, bringing my stiff back to the headboard.

"I'm fine." I smile thinly.

"But you're not, are you?" He raises an eyebrow. "You can't save everyone, Ella."

"I know but..."

"No, you don't know. You're strong and brave, also stubborn at times, and I've never met anyone quite like you before. But you can't save everyone that's in trouble. You need take care of yourself too." His dark gaze meets mine.

"It's my fault." My voice breaks as I replay the memories of rotting corpses. My friends, my loved ones. Looking down at the silky bed sheets, I finally bring my gaze up to meet those soft, brown eyes that regard me intently.

"What's your fault?" Troy looks quizzically at me.

"This whole thing is my fault."

"I don't think the zombie apocalypse is your fault." I see a twitch of a smile approach his lips and I laugh softly. There's that playful side of him again. "Seriously though, Ella, you've got to stop trying to protect everyone. We're a team. We stick together." He smiles at me while I look down at the bed once again.

"I don't try to save everyone," I mumble.

"Yes, you do."

I sigh and look up at him. He has dark circles outlining the memories that haunt him, the memories that are sketched deep within our souls, the memories that are carved across our hearts. Too damaged to hope, too damaged to scream. All we can do is journey on and wish.

As I get drawn back towards Troy, I notice that his dark, brown hair is pushed slightly over to the side. I notice the small, copper strands running riot against the darkness. The moonlight bounces off his tanned skin, his raw strength highlighted in the deep, breathless movement of his chest. The steady rhythm of his breathing calms me instantly and I feel safe, protected. The feeling is new to me.

"You going to stay up here forever?" He smiles, cocking his head to the side.

"I was just clearing my head." I start to get up, pushing the soft blankets away from my shivering body.

"I know the feeling." He runs a hand through his hair as he notices the goose bumps rising on my forearms.

He immediately takes off his grey jumper without hesitation and hands it to me — the warm material brushing against my fingertips, the heavenly scent of Troy lingering over each thread of cotton. I quickly shrug it on and feel the chill of night slip away. The whistling wind sneaking through the small crack in the window distracts me. As the breeze grows stronger, the red curtains float through the air marking shadows over my skin.

"Are Zoe and Dale doing okay?" I turn my attention back to

Troy.

"Yeah, they're fine. Zoe's quite attached to you, you know." He smiles.

"Well, she needs someone she can trust. Someone that will be there for her." I continually say to myself that I will protect her at whatever cost, but I don't know how much of that is true. What if I can't save her, like Terry? Like Jim? Like Leila?

"I know. We'll all protect her. We will all protect you too." He gently rises off the bed. "You going to come down? I think Zoe wants to hear a story before she goes to bed." He chuckles and I smile.

"I'll be right down," I say, watching him leave the room.

I pull the last of the blankets off me and check my feet over. Huge, red blisters cover them, seeping out blood. They look pretty bad. It's hard to walk on them without wincing in pain, but they're the least of my worries. I walk into the en-suite bathroom. The walls are pale beige with small flowers draped over the ceiling. I check my reflection in the bathroom mirror. The mirror itself has a huge crack through the middle and sink is pretty dirty too. I watch my lifeless blonde hair cascade down past my shoulders. The scrapes and dried blood staining my cheeks. The raw cut scraped across my bottom lip. The streaks of mud and dirt layering on my neck. The haunting dark eyes of a girl I don't recognise stare back at me. I can only sigh at my reflection. I'm not the girl I used to be, nor will I ever be the same again.

I notice a small cabinet above the sink and I raid the cupboard, grabbing what looks like antiseptic cream. After cleaning up a bit, I rub the cream onto the blisters on my feet and pull my dirt-stained socks up to cover them. I stand up, wincing from the pain, careful not to put too much weight on the balls of my feet. When I'm finished, I walk down the stairs to find Dale, Troy, and Zoe sitting on the pale pink sofa. Dale smiles at me as I make my way down.

"You feeling okay?" Troy asks, with a worried look.

"Yeah, I just needed a minute." I brush him off and look at Zoe. Her hair is matted and covered with mud. Her eyes are outlined with dark circles and I can see a new bandage wrapped around her leg. She looks up at me from where she lays against Troy's shoulder.

"Don't you look tired." I say, crouching down beside her.

"Ella, are we going to be okay?" She asks, barely awake. I look up at Dale and his face remains blank.

"I hope so," I say. She smiles, gripping my hand as she gently falls asleep.

Troy lets her sleep against him for a while until we retire to our own rooms. He picks her up as if she weighs no more than a breadcrumb and carries her into our bedroom, laying her down on the bed. I climb into the other side of the bed and lay silently beside her.

"Night, Ella." Troy smiles and shuts the door behind him. I listen to the soft breathing coming from Zoe and I start to drift off myself.

I wake up to the sound of a gunshot. I hastily bolt upright and look out the cracked window. The wind still whistles through the small hole, creating an icy chill that invades the room. It's still dark out. Maybe I just imagined it, which wouldn't surprise me with all my nightmares lately. Zoe sleeps soundlessly next to me so she can't have heard. I start to hear footsteps outside our bedroom and decide to scope it out. I walk towards the door, stepping over my shoes and jacket that I've discarded on the floor and creak the handle open slowly. I shiver and hold my arms around myself as I'm reminded that I'm only wearing a strappy top and a pair of linen shorts — pyjamas that I've stolen from one of the many drawers in the main bedroom. I wish I could take them with me but our backpacks are already too heavy. I continue to follow the footsteps and start to see a figure at the end of the hallway, holding a flashlight.

"Troy?" I say, squinting my eyes. He shines the flashlight directly at me, momentarily blinding me. I immediately hold my hand in front of my face as he shines it away.

"Sorry," he apologises.

"What are you doing up?" I ask, walking over to him.

"I could say the same thing to you." He raises an eyebrow. Just then, I realise he is only wearing his boxer shorts and I have to quickly divert my eyes away from his rippling, muscular chest and broad shoulders. I feel my mouth dry slightly and struggle for words.

"I heard a gunshot," I say, finally. A small grin emits on Troy's face when he catches me gazing at him and I scowl at his expression.

"I heard it too and was just going to check it out. Dale is still asleep." He rolls his eyes.

I laugh quietly and we walk down the stairs into the dark shadows, with the only light coming from the glow of the flashlight. The atmosphere is silent as we walk out the front door. The cold night immediately wraps its way around us, sending chills up my spine. I bundle my arms around myself, trying to keep warm, searching for the strange noise. Troy shines the flashlight around, but neither of us can see anything, so we do a few laps around the house, but our tired eyes can't find where the sound came from.

"I guess it was quite far away." Troy yawns and walks back into the house.

"I guess," I mumble, not satisfied about our safety.

I do a few more laps around the house, hiding in the shadows for the sound to come back. I sit cross-legged out in the cold with my arms wrapped around myself. I will not leave here until I know what the sound was. I won't risk everyone's lives again, even if it takes all night. I know I heard a gunshot. I sit on an old wicker chair in the middle of the wooden porch so I can see out for miles. I sit there, searching for danger until my eyelids start to close, huddling up tightly in the chair.

"You're still out here? *Jesus,* Ella! You're freezing!" Troy wakes me by touching my frozen arm. I open my eyes and see the sunrise has come up over the mountains in the distance. I look up to the beautiful colours filling the sky. A warm sunny glow travels up the porch and over my body as the sun rises higher into the dreary clouds.

"Ella, are you *crazy*? You stayed out here all night?" Troy's expression is one of concern and blazing anger.

"I wasn't going in, until it was safe," I say, rubbing my eyes.

"That was really stupid. You could of caught pneumonia or been attacked by those creatures!" Troy helps pull me off the chair.

"I don't care. I need to keep everyone safe," I snap at him.

"It's not down to you to save everyone," Troy snaps back, his eyes flaring with annoyance.

"Yes it is. I cannot be responsible for any more deaths!" I shout. He looks momentarily shocked at my outburst.

"Ella," he lowers his voice. "You're not responsible for any deaths."

"Yes, I am. I couldn't save them!" I run my hands through my matted morning hair.

"Ella..."

"No, don't tell me that none of this is my fault. Just leave it!" I crumble onto the steps of the porch, trying to calm myself down before I do something stupid.

After a few seconds, Troy comes over and sits next to me. I realise that I still have my strappy top and shorts on from last night, and it was a stupid idea to stay outside in the cold, but I can't think straight. The horrors of this world still whirl around in my head and I have to do everything I can to protect my friends. They're all I have left.

"Ella, I know you've seen some horrible things and I know you have been through a lot, but you can't save everyone." Troy looks at me with his golden brown eyes.

"I know." Although I agree with him, it won't stop me from protecting them all. I will do everything I can. Nobody else is going to die, not on my watch.

"Can you come in now and get warm?" Troy holds out his hand and I take it.

Dale runs to the front door, out of breath, and leans on the doorframe. I furrow my brows at him and so does Troy.

"Have either of you seen, Zoe?" He looks wildly between us. I look to Troy and he shakes his head so Dale runs back inside.

"Zoe?" he shouts. But he gets no reply.

"Dale, what's happening?" I walk in and he stops in his tracks. He looks around at us.

"Zoe wasn't in your room when I went to wake you both up, and she isn't in the house anywhere. I thought she might be with you." He runs his hands through his dark, dishevelled hair.

Just great.

CHAPTER 17

"SHE ISN'T ANYWHERE?" TROY STARTS to look around aimlessly.

"No, genius," Dale snaps, running upstairs again. Paying no attention to Dale, Troy shouts out Zoe's name and I do the same.

After ten minutes of searching every room, corridor, and the whole back garden of the house, we still remain clueless. I've decided that it will be a lot faster to split up outside searching for her. I know we shouldn't split up but we need to find her, we need to cover as much ground as we possibly can. Dale is searching the other houses and Troy is searching the left end of the street. I, on the other hand, am searching the right side. Brick buildings stand tall around me. Old shop signs hang lifelessly, covered in bloodied handprints. Glass doors are broken and jagged shards litter the deserted walkways. A few factories come into view while I continue to walk down the cracked road, the tarmac painful against my raging blisters. I wince as I walk through the shadows created by even more factories. This part of town is quiet, not even a single whistle of wind disturbing the eerie essence. Before we left the house, I threw on a black top and trousers and pulled on my boots. I also grabbed my sword just in case.

"Zoe?" I shout, my voice echoing through the deserted town surrounding me. I kick a few dusty rocks on the ground as they roll off the road and land in a small, dark pit dug next to a factory building.

The big, iron letters hang from the doorway, many already smashed to the floor. I walk over, following the rocks and find myself peering into the dark hole. I can't see much so I squint my eyes in the darkness. *Why is there a hole here?* My feet balance on the edge of the crumbling rocks, each one falling into the unknown.

"Zoe?" I call down into the hole.

All of a sudden I feel an unexpected gust of wind, an almighty strength that causes me to completely lose my balance. I try to stay upright, I try to grip onto the side but the wind is too strong and I feel myself begin to fall. I fall desperately down into the darkness. The unknown swallowing me whole. The last thing I see is the small patch of light growing narrower by the second.

"Mummy?"

"Don't worry, honey. It will only hurt for second." A tall dark-haired woman stands next to her daughter, her daughter the exact picture of her own features — small pointed nose, flushed cheeks, and dotted brown freckles.

The woman holds out a sharp needle filled with a blue liquid.

"I don't like it when we do this." The little girl fidgets in her chair. Her arms placed flat against the wooden arms and her long, blonde hair falling in curls just past her shoulders.

"I know, I know, honey. Please keep still. This is for your own good." The woman carefully pierces the needle into the little girl's pale arm.

"I love you, my little Rememdium."

"I love you too, Mummy." The little girl shudders as the liquid fills her veins, fills her heart with a new sense of control.

"I will always love you, no matter what." The woman's face flashes before the little girl's green eyes as she slumps back in the chair and falls into a deep sleep.

My eyes open to darkness. Complete and utter darkness. The small patch of light spotlighting the ground on which I've fallen. As I look up, the opening seems miles away. I place my hands on the soggy ground, mud and earth caressing my fingertips. *Where am I?* Getting up off the floor, I dust off the mud from my clothes and find a lone match on the ground. Lighting it against the walls, I find a small stick and light the end carefully. A blast of fire highlights a narrow tunnel ahead and I follow the pathway, seeing as I don't really have a choice of climbing out any other way.

The rocks crumble above my head, each one hitting me in the face as I walk through the underground tunnel. The fire on my stick growing hotter by the second. I start to run, to find a way out before the wooden stick burns out completely.

"Zoe?" I shout. There may be a tiny chance that she's down here.

No answer. Great.

A doorway finally comes into view, the handle made with gold and shaped as a man's head, a large metal ring piercing through his nose. His eyes are painted with a deep red, probably to scare people away. People like me, who have fallen down the hole in the ground. *Please tell me that there isn't a Wonderland waiting for me on the other side of this door.* I take a deep breath and push the golden handles with all my force. The doors creak open with a loud smash against the dark walls. I was wrong. It's not Wonderland waiting for me after all, it is worse.

Cages. Lots of cages. Massive metal containers, iron bars. The smell of rot explodes through my senses. I almost faint from the sight. Zombies. Zombies everywhere. All of them hungry, frothing at the mouth as they try to eat one another. They are trapped inside cages. Like a prison. Innocent lives that have been transformed into monsters are now locked up in this *hell.* I stalk into the room, my mouth gaping with every new sight. Torches hang on the walls and groups of footprints layer the ground. As I look into each cage, I see bones, rotting corpses, skulls, and flies circling the diseased stench. *Why are zombies down here? Why are they locked up? Is someone keeping them as pets*? I shake my head with all of the unanswered questions.

I look down at the skulls again. Human skulls. Mainly small, from children perhaps? Zoe's picture appears in my head and I have to shake it away before I start to cry. There's no way she would have been zombie food. She's stronger than that.

I start to hear voices so I quickly dart into the shadows, next to a metal cage. A whole mass of zombies turn towards me and I immediately regret my action. They all run for me, their arms draping out of the metal bars. They try to claim me, to possess me, but I'm too far away from their reach.

"Excellent work here, Percy." A man walks out of a door on the left, followed by a group of army men.

The man himself wears a dark blue suit, buttoned up with

sparkling silver studs. He carries a brown briefcase in his right hand and I'm immediately drawn to his watch. The gold-plated numbers surrounded by sapphire gems and ruby stones. Where have I seen that before? I crease my brows. I can't see the man's face due to the metal cage blocking my view. I can't exactly jump out and surprise attack them because that would only result in me being the zombie's main course. I shudder at the thought.

"Thank you, sir. You'll have your results by Friday." The main army man states and leads him out another doorway on the right.

As the group disappears, I take in one last sight of the zombie cages and desperately hope that Zoe hasn't seen any of this. I hope no one *ever* sees any of this. How on earth will I ever explain it to the others, that's if they'll even believe me? That's if I ever make it out of here. I follow the group down another tunnel, carefully following the light in front of me. I stay well back in case they change their course of direction. I'm too far away to hear what's being said, but I can almost make out small words here and there.

"Tests…are…never…why…follow…results…blood…escape…Society."

I stop abruptly when I hear the mention of The Society. *Do more people know about it than we originally thought? Is it a bad idea to go there?* Suddenly the group stops before a metal ladder on the wall. We've reached a dead-end. *Well, great.*

"Good luck with your research. You're welcome here anytime, sir." The army man stands proud and pats the man wearing the suit on the shoulder.

"I will be in touch," the other man replies, carefully climbing up the metal ladder.

The group of army men turn towards me and I panic. *Crap!* They're coming back this way. I run back down the tunnel, entering the room of cages once again. I hide in the corner, out of view, and watch the group disperse around the room. I exhale and hold my knees as they shake with uncertainty. The main army man calls out to the others, grabbing a spear off the horrifying wall of weapons. He holds it out in front of him as one of the cage doors cranks open. He walks into the cage with the zombies running for him. He smacks them away using the spear and finally herds two diseased monsters, the other men chaining them to the ground. I watch the horrible scene but decide that Zoe is not down here, and if she was, she must have escaped by now. Leaving the room behind, I run down the tunnel and find the metal ladder before me. Climbing up for what seems like hours, I find myself back in the street surrounded by factories.

How will I ever explain this? The disturbing hell, underground. *Are they testing those zombies? Why?* I curse to myself for not knowing anything more. More unanswered questions whirl through my head, joining the others. I need to focus on finding Zoe.

"Zoe?" I shout. My feet throb with every step but I keep my eyes peeled, watching for any movement around me. The remains of houses are getting worse the further I walk. Doors are hanging off their hinges, and most of the roof tiles are missing or have collapsed altogether. The cracked pavement I walk on is covered in blood and raw ligaments from rotting bodies, but I choose to ignore them.

I check over my shoulder but the dark pit is long gone behind me, along with the zombie hell. *Maybe I should turn back?* I don't want to go too far away from the others, so I start to turn around when a scream fills the air. Spinning towards the noise, wearing a wide-eyed expression, I run towards it.

"Zoe?" I shout.

Another terrified scream echoes through the town, so I run as fast as I can towards the sound. Dust from the ground fills the air behind me as it swirls up, causing a foggy cloud to follow me. Suddenly a gunshot goes off and I stop. Something hits the ground next to me and I run over to it cautiously. A bullet. *Someone's shooting at me*? Another gunshot goes off, louder than the last, and an excruciating pain rips through my side. I scream out in agony. Shock and confusion flickers through my mind, I start to run, holding pressure to my side, but the pain is too much.

I continue to run as fast as I can and hide behind a broken down, metal truck. I take my hand away from my side and see deep, red blood seeping out. I lift up my soaked-through top to see my injury. The bullet has hit me in my side but luckily it hasn't gone in too deep. I clench my eyes shut from the pain and wince as I check it over. All the blood loss starts to make me feel dizzy and uneasy. *No! I must find Zoe!*

Quickly I pull my top back down and grab my sword, my bloody hand slips on the handle and it costs me another scream to pick it up off the ground. My heart thumps slowly, counting down the seconds. Seconds that I don't have. If the gunshots and screaming haven't attracted zombies by now, the smell of my blood probably will. I stumble out from behind the truck and quickly sprint towards a dark alleyway hiding between two houses. Slamming my back against the alley walls, I grit my teeth in agony. Enduring the pain, I look out into the street cautiously, but I can't see any movement. *Who's shooting at me and where is Zoe?* I want to shout her name but I'm afraid my attackers will shoot again. I can't take another shot. I hold my hand to my side, trying to stop the quick flow of blood from escaping my body. I just need to carry on until I find her. Another scream interrupts the deathly silence and I spring to my feet, my energy quickly crumbling by the minute. Sprinting over the hard, rocky ground that was once a busy main road, I run with all the strength left in me, every fibre of pain I'm willing to sacrifice for Zoe. Falling over my feet several times, I pick myself back up.

Finally, I stop at a building in front of me and hide amongst the shadows. A few voices come from inside and I crouch down against a damp, brick wall. A few old, battered windows are dotted around with wooden bars blocking the view from inside. I find a little gap and rub the dust from the glass, trying to peer in. The dark room is empty, so I move on. I run over to another window, trying to stay out of sight. I rub the dirt from the glass using my jacket sleeve, and peer in. The sight shocks me. Zoe hides underneath a tower of barrels. One of them is leaking and is slowly filling the ground with a red liquid. I presume they are wine crates.

My eyes widen and I wince again as my side loses more and more blood. I keep pressure on it, taking a deep breath. All I want to do is scream her name so she knows she's safe. Deciding my body can't take much more, I smash the windowpane using the handle of my sword and jump through, trying not to get any glass stuck in my side. I quickly run behind the barrels alongside Zoe and she looks up, surprised and relieved.

"Zoe, what…" But she covers my mouth with her hand before I can finish, putting a finger to her lips.

I huddle next to her as loud, thundering footsteps come from above us. They get louder and louder. My heartbeat thumps as I continue to hold my hand against my side. Zoe has taken her hand away from my mouth, but we remain silent while the footsteps grow louder. Crouching down in the dark, we are out of sight. *Why on earth is Zoe in here anyway?* I look at her determined little face as she listens for the footsteps. They slowly fade away and she starts to whisper to me.

"We need to go, now!" She starts crawling ahead of me.

The pain is slowly spreading through my body and I start to feel lightheaded. It flows through every vein, every heartbeat, until my head also starts to throb. I follow her, crawling through the shadows together. A few voices come from above us, but we keep moving ahead towards the broken glass on the floor. We get up and step over the jagged edges that are waiting to pierce our flesh, to taste our blood. Suddenly a loud gunshot goes off behind us and we both freeze.

"I've got them," a husky voice comes from behind us. I slowly turn around to see a slimy grin on a man's face a few meters away. Zoe's eyes widen in fear as she notices the gun he holds by his side. I have time to get Zoe out of here but he might shoot.

"Who are you?" I stall him.

He starts laughing and I hold out my sword. His dirty blonde hair and his dark eyes make him quite attractive — but his evil grin makes me think otherwise.

"You have two options," he says, smiling. "You can both escape and give me a game of hunting." He points to his gun. "Or you can come with me, willingly." His grin widens and I have no idea what to do. If we escape, we might end up dead anyway, but we could be dead either way.

"So it was you who shot me?" I ask, holding my side with one hand. Zoe looks at my injury in shock and then looks at the man in front of us, anger blazing in her eyes.

"You could say that. Couldn't have you getting away now, could we?" He laughs again. My mind whirls with what to do as I start to drop my sword down a little. But as I do, a knife whirls past me through the air and stabs the man in his chest. He stumbles backward in pain.

"You bitch!" he shouts. I turn around wide-eyed at Zoe, but am a little impressed at the same time.

"Go!" Zoe shouts. I give her a leg up out the window, and when she lands on the ground, a stampede of footsteps run down from upstairs. I climb out the window after her but midway, a hand grabs my ankle. Looking down, panicking, I see the man has a tight grip around my leg. His chest is bleeding as he slowly pulls the knife out of his flesh, ready to dig it into my own skin.

"Ella, come on!" Zoe shouts from the other side of the window.

"Get off!" I scream, trying to kick and squirm out of his clutch. I finally get my leg free and kick him in the head, causing him to shout out in pain.

I jump out the window as a few edges of glass pierce into the palm of my hands. I wince while I pull the shards of glass out of my skin. We start to run away from the building, with booming gunshots echoing behind us. Zoe can barely walk on her bandaged leg, and stumbles over rocks, but tries her best to stay upright. I try to carry her but my side is burning with scorching agony. I can't take my hand away or else I'll lose too much blood.

"Keep running!" I shout over the noise.

I take Zoe's hand with my free arm and she runs as fast as her little legs can carry her. Her face winces in pain when she stumbles yet again. Sweat slides down my forehead while I try to get us to safety. My side is still throbbing so I push even more pressure onto it with my bloodstained hand. I try to cope with the pain, but my head starts to feel dizzy. A few bullets hit the ground next to us, making Zoe jump and land into my side. I clench my jaw shut to stop myself from screaming. Zoe notices my reaction and looks up with a horrified expression. She's obviously noticed the blood leaking and soaking through my top.

"Just keeping going!" I say, repeating my parents' own words.

She starts to speed up and pulls at my hand. I realise I'm starting to slow down from the pain as my knees hit the dusty floor.

"Ella, come on!" Zoe screams, more gunshots sounding behind us.

I try to control my breathing, but the agony travels up my body. I look down and take my hand away, noticing the red bloodied mess getting worse. The skin is red raw and the pain is excruciating. I curse under my breath, pulling my top back down to cover it.

"Ella, we need to get out of here!" Zoe shouts, trying to pull me up.

"Just go without me." Hot tears stream down my face.

"No, Ella! Come on!" Her watering eyes are filled with fear, worry, and terror that she might have to leave me.

"Just go!" I cry harder as I lean forwards, trying to block out the pain from my side. I start to gag, my mouth dry, while my stomach spasms out of control. I hunch over, trying not to throw up.

"Ella, *no!*" Zoe tries to pull my hand again. I hear a low growl behind us and Zoe's eyes widen even more.

Her eyes dart between me and the monster approaching us. I suddenly want to grab her and stop the mistake she's about to make, but I can't move. The pain has frozen me to the spot. When I look up, I see Zoe stumbling towards the beast behind me.

"Zoe! NOOOOO!" I scream, trying to stand up, pushing the pain away. I manage to drag myself up on both legs, stumbling around from exhaustion, my vision blurry and my eyes starting to close. I turn around and see Zoe approaching the lone zombie with a wild look in her eye.

"*NOOO!*" I scream.

She is five feet away from the horrible monster when a pair of strong arms grab her and lift her up from the ground. Dale runs toward me with her as Troy snaps the zombie's neck and stabs it with his own sword.

"Ella, run!" Dale shouts, as he's sprinting over to me.

"I-I c-can't," I say, looking up at him with tear-soaked eyes. His eyes widen as he looks at my side.

"Ella, I..." Dale holds Zoe in his arms, not knowing what to do, and stops next to me. Suddenly a pair of muscular arms lift me effortlessly off the floor and I look up to see Troy's worried expression.

"Let's go!" Dale runs off with Zoe and Troy follows.

I scream in pain as my side rubs against Troy's hard chest. My head throbs. I can feel myself leaving the world but I keep my eyes open as long as I can. But soon, the world fades away into blackness and the pain disappears. I may not be in Wonderland, but I'm sure in Zombieland.

My eyes flutter open and I find myself lying on my back. My body quivers and aches from the agonising torture, the pain shooting up and down each one of my veins. My back arches as I lose control, the burning sensation taking over. I scream, my throat dry, letting out everything within me. I never thought that anything could hurt this bad. I feel like my insides have been ripped out one by one, my skin being slowly burnt to ash. Every single fibre of energy erupts from my lungs and I scream so loud, my ears ring with madness.

"Leave me alone!" I shout out, my head dizzy. My blurred vision spins me around the room. Every speck of sanity seems to ripple with uneasiness and exhaustion.

"What are you doing to her?" a deep voice shouts, almost a plea. I open my eyes again to see the blurry, faint outline of Troy standing by my side.

"I'm trying to help her. Goddammit!" Another voice comes from my left. I try to lift my head but my side screams with the intense agony once again and I shout out from the blinding torture.

"You're hurting her!" Troy shouts.

"It's deep and I'm trying to clean it out!" the other voice yells back.

My body shakes as I scream out again.

"Get off me!"

"Ella, calm down! I'm trying to help." I look up to see Dale's concerned expression. He sits, calmly attending to my injury. Troy paces up and down at the side of my bed. My vision is still blurry as I clench my eyes shut from the torment.

"I'm going to start to clean it now, Ella," Dale informs me, and I nod weakly.

A sudden fire blazes through me and I curse, screaming out.

"Hurry up! She's in pain!" Troy roars, raking his strong hands through his hair in distress.

Suddenly the pain becomes too much and I can't take any-more. My body falls limp and soon enough, I pass out into the darkness.

The grotesque creature runs at Leila. Mangled diseased skin hangs from its face. Its bottom lip is missing, along with most of its teeth, as yellow drool seeps out from its neck. Bones pierce straight through its rotting flesh and most of them stick out through its chest. It growls and lunges. It's speed, as quick as lightning as it grabs onto Leila's tiny ankle.

"Leila, NOOO!" I scream, but nothing escapes my lungs.

"Leila!" I scream again, but I have no voice. I try to run to her but my feet are stuck. I can't move them. The monster rips at her legs as she screams out in terror.

"Ella, help me!" she cries.

I use all my strength to try and move, but I can't. My feet are glued to the floor and I'm starting to sink into the ground. The mud-dy pit consuming me, possessing me.

"Leila!" I scream, but again no sound comes out.

"Ella! Help…" Leila's voice breaks in agony as it echoes throughout the foggy air.

My body is halfway into the ground when the creature grips onto Leila's pale arm. It bears its sharp teeth and locks its target, going in for a bite.

"NOOO!" I scream, as I disappear into the rocky ground.

The last thing I see is the hopeless fear in Leila's golden brown eyes.

"Ella? Are you okay?"

My eyelids flutter open to find Dale's dark features assessing me, his jaw clenched shut with slightly more stubble than before. As I rub my eyes, I can see a slight relieved look on his face.

"Dale?" My throat feels dry.

"Thank God, Ella." He exhales and puts a reassuring hand on my arm. He's dressed head-to-toe in blood-soaked clothes. His arm is covered in cuts and scrapes and he has a dark bruise on his cheek, just under his right eye.

"W-what's going on?" I ask, confused. I try to sit up but my side stings, throwing me back down into a sleeping position. I gaze down at my body to find a tight bandage tied around my lower stomach.

"You were in a lot of pain. I cleaned your wound and stitched it up for you." His expression is grim, but he looks relieved to see me awake.

"How long have I been out?"

"Not long, a few hours." He sits up in his chair.

"A few hours? That's too long. We don't have that kind of time to spare." I start to panic as a look of amusement lights up in Dale's eyes.

"Ella, calm down. You need to rest."

"Have you been here the whole time?"

He nods slowly. "Yeah, you've been screaming in your sleep. Troy's been in and out. He's been very worried about you. He's been looking after Zoe, but it's proving to be very hard to keep her away from this room." He smiles weakly.

"Thank you," I say, smiling back at him.

"I…we…" he corrects himself. "We can't lose you, Ella."

I smile as Troy walks into the room with a scowling Zoe. She pushes past him when she sees me and Dale.

"Ella!" Zoe runs over and throws her arms around me. I laugh but it hurts my side.

"I was so worried. I thought you were going to *die!* And then *he* wouldn't let me in. I even snuck past him a few times but he's very fast." She glares at Troy as he rolls his eyes. "I thought I was going to lose you. I heard you screaming." Her eyes start to water and I wipe away her leaking tears with my own hand.

"Hey. It's okay. I'm fine now," I reply, weakly.

She smiles but she doesn't take her arms away from me. Smiling down at Zoe, I eventually bring my gaze up to Troy. He watches me closely from the doorway. I see something in his eyes. Something different, something soft and almost caring.

"I'm glad you're awake." He has large, dark circles under his eyes and his hair is standing up on end. His shirt is equally covered in blood and his shoulders are tattooed with scratches. I frown at them as he walks over slowly. Lifting the duvet up from the other side of the room, he places it over my shivering body. Zoe squeezes my hand tightly, having no intention of leaving me.

"We'll let you get some rest, Ella." Troy looks toward Zoe, raising a dark eyebrow. His expression hardens as if challenging her to argue with him again.

Zoe just frowns. She's a very strong, young girl. And unlike me, she's not intimidated by Troy. *No matter how menacing his expression is.*

"It's okay, Zoe. Troy will look after you, but I do need to rest." My eyelids are starting to close as we speak.

Zoe sighs, looking between me and Troy. She finally gives in and follows Troy towards the bedroom door. Troy gently pushes Zoe into the hallway and hesitates, waiting for Dale to follow.

"You two should get some rest. I'm staying here to make sure Ella's okay." Dale doesn't take his tired eyes away from me.

I see a small flare of annoyance in Troy's expression. He looks from me to Dale as if contemplating whether to actually leave us alone together. But someone needs to keep an eye on Zoe, so he leaves without another word.

"You okay?" Dale asks as Troy shuts the door behind them, with more force than necessary.

I nod and lay my head back on the pillow.

"Where are we?"

"When you passed out, we ran back to the house. No one followed us. We haven't heard any more zombies or gunshots for a while. We were so worried that we carried you up here and tried to attend to your side." He smiles sympathetically. "I'm guessing you got shot?"

"Yeah, those men. They shot me as I ran to save Zoe," I reply, noticing a flicker of anger cross Dale's face.

"I should've come with you. We shouldn't have split up." He shakes his head.

"Hey, it's okay." I touch his arm with my hand to reassure him. "They might have shot you too, if you had."

"It still wouldn't have got you." His dark eyes search mine.

I sigh as a few seconds of silence airs between us. *Why did they shoot me? Why was Zoe in that building in the first place?*

"Zoe threw a knife at one of the men attacking me." I look up at him.

Dale immediately looks shocked and then laughs a little. "What?" he asks.

"She saw my injury. Next thing I knew, a knife was flying through the air." I smile at the impressive nine-year-old we have with us.

Dale laughs and shakes his head. "She really is something."

I start to close my eyes, smiling. But I quickly open them again, feeling rude to ignore him when he worked so hard on my stomach.

"Ella, it's okay. Get some rest," he smiles. I lay my head back down on the pillow and it's not long before I drift off again.

I open my eyes to find Troy at my bedside. He sits next to the bed on an old, wooden rocking chair. His head is resting on his flexed arms. Dark, intimidating circles have formed around his eyes and he wears a new, clean set of black leather trousers. His waterproof jacket is hung over the end of the bed. *Has he been here the whole time I was sleeping?* I try to hoist myself up a bit, careful not to disturb him. He probably hasn't had a good night's rest in a while. I lift myself up but cry out in agony when a bolt of pain travels up my body. Troy immediately jumps up at my side.

"Ella, are you alright?" He looks around, trying to piece together my sudden outburst.

"Yeah, I'm fine. It's just my side." I clench my eyes shut as the pain starts to fade away.

"Will you just rest and stop trying to move?" Troy closes his eyes in frustration.

"Sorry," I say, quietly.

"Ella, it's not your fault," he sighs. "I'm sorry." He starts to sit up in his chair and fixes his gaze on me. "You'll be able to move soon, just rest for now." The deep brown of his eyes calm me and I lay my head back down. I can't help but drift off once again.

I wake up to an empty room. I look out the window and see daylight streaming in. *How long have I been asleep?* We can't waste any more time with me stuck in bed. For all I know, I've been sleeping for days. I sit up slowly and wince from the pain as I carefully drag myself out of bed. I stare down at my side. The bandage covering most of my lower stomach is tied neatly around my waist. I gently pull on my underwear over the bandage. Discarding the nightgown I wear, I throw it on the floor. I've never been a tidy person. Once I'm set, I stand up and grab a spare top out of my backpack, which just happens to be on the tallest shelf in the room. The tight leather clings to my skin, which doesn't really help my injury, but I don't have anything else. I check the bandage around my stomach before pulling my top down to cover it. Next, I pull my trousers on and walk towards the door. My feet burn with every step. Each blister stings in a horrifying rhythm. I shut my eyes, blocking out the pain. Both my feet and my side can wait. We need to get somewhere safe. Hiding out here isn't doing us any good. Soon the smell of fresh blood will attract more zombies and we will be surrounded.

I open the bedroom door and gradually make my way to the end of the upstairs hallway. I hold my side, throbbing every time I move. I look up to find all the walls are covered in torn pictures and paintings. A picture of a family is smashed on the floor and I bend down to pick it up. I clench my eyes shut from the shooting flames in my stomach while I get back up slowly. I don't want to rip the stitching.

A family of five fill the frame. A young girl with her two brothers, and her parents. All these innocent people are dying because of this virus. Happy families are being destroyed. I put the picture back on the wall, hanging it neatly on a small nail. I finally make my way downstairs to find three faces looking up at me in surprise.

"Ella?" Dale holds a spoon full of cereal halfway up to his mouth, staring open-mouthed.

"Hi." I smile as I head towards them. Zoe beams a smile at me, but Troy narrows his eyes.

"You should be in bed," he mumbles, taking a spoonful out if his own bowl of cereal.

"We found food in the cupboard!" Zoe skips over to me and hands me a cracked china bowl.

"Thanks," I smile, taking a seat at the table.

"Are you feeling any better?" Dale scans me over.

"Yes. Much." I grab the box of cereal off the table and start to pour out each grain to fill the china bowl. It's been a while since I've eaten anything. My stomach grumbles in appreciation as I munch down the first spoonful.

"We don't have any milk but at least it's food." Dale smiles. "Be careful though, Ella. Don't eat too much because your body might not be able to take it."

I nod and eat half the bowl.

"When are we heading out?" I ask, and I get three blank stares. I guess they haven't discussed it yet.

"Ella…" Troy starts, but Dale interrupts.

"I don't think it's a good idea with your injury and all. You've been out for a few days." He looks away.

A few days? Warning bells suddenly fill my head, the red alarms swirling through my mind. A few days here is long enough. We can't possibly stay here any longer without running into any more trouble.

"I'm fine. We can't stay here much longer." I raise my eyebrows. They all know I'm right.

"Ella, we can't have you traveling around with a gunshot wound," Troy eventually says.

"Look, I'm fine. We need to leave here before something else happens." I drop my half-eaten bowl of cereal into the sink and walk back towards the table.

"Ella, we can't…" Dale starts.

"Look, we've been here long enough. I'm really grateful that you are all worried about me, but I'm fine. I don't know what I'd do without any of you and I don't want to find out, so we really need to leave."

"Fine." Troy dumps his bowl in the sink and walks upstairs.

"Ignore him, Ella. I'm just glad you're feeling better," Dale says, smiling at me and picking up Zoe, tickling her. She giggles as she runs over to hug me.

"I'm glad you're okay, Ella." Her little face brightens up and she heads upstairs.

"Are you sure you want to leave?" Dale looks uncertain.

"Yes. If we stay here, we will all end up dead one way or another," I sigh.

He smiles warily. After a few seconds of silence, I look at him. "Thank you."

"I…I couldn't just let you die." Dale looks down at the floor.

"Dale, thank you. I can never repay you and Troy enough for saving my life…and Zoe's." I smile warmly at him.

He and Troy both saved us from the zombie and the shooting brigade. I will never be able to repay them, but I will do whatever I can to keep them all alive. We need each other.

"How did you know what to do?" I ask. "With my injury, I mean?"

"I was studying medicine before the virus started to spread." He shrugs.

I giggle at the thought of him studying medicine after seeing him slice zombies in half.

"Thank you."

"Stop saying thank you, Ella," Dale laughs.

“Sorry. Even if you can’t practice medicine anymore, I think you may have a future in zombie slaying.” I grin.

“You’re not so bad yourself,” he smirks.

I laugh. As I look up, I start to see a figure moving behind us in the shadows.

“Dale, watch out!” I shout. But it’s too late. A man runs at us and stabs Dale in the arm.

Chapter 18

DALE CURSES OUT IN PAIN. The man takes the knife back in his hand and I get a slight glimpse into his eyes. Silvery eyes that send chills up my ice-cold spine. My mind immediately goes back to where I found Zoe. *It's the same man!* The man that shot me. The man Zoe threw a knife at. *Now he's here.* He's dressed in all black and wears a mask covering most of face. His hand is covered in Dale's blood as he backs up towards the back door. Working with what I've got, I quickly grab the nearest thing to me and end up with a saucepan. I frown. It's better than nothing, I suppose. Dale holds his arm and stumbling towards the countertops, he grabs a china plate from one of the cupboards, avoiding another blow in the shoulder from the knife man.

A few other men charge through the open back door as the wind whistles in through the kitchen. They all charge, shouting instructions to one another as their beady eyes latch onto us. Each man wears a mask, scary Halloween masks. Two clowns with blood dripping from their mouths, a skeleton with dark hollow eyes and yellow rotting bones, and my favourite has got to be the drooling zombie masks. I don't waste a second and smack the first man over the head using the saucepan, but he continually runs at Dale again. He obviously sees Dale as the bigger threat or he would've lunged for me too by now. The man freezes when I raise the saucepan to hit him again and turns around to face me. His eyes are blazing with fury, locking his target. I smile sweetly as I ram the saucepan straight into his face. He roars with pain, his body slackening against the countertops. He catches his hand on the edge of a knife and screams out. Within his anger, he charges blind, aiming for me. Dale quickly smashes a plate over his head, creating a slash in his skull, and pushes him to the floor. I quickly jump over the two of them, cursing out from the pain of my side. Gritting my teeth, I'm ready for the others. I stand in front the other three men that face us. Each have a gleaming sword and a gun, plus I'm greatly outnumbered. I'm also injured.

They all wear the same green uniform like we saw back in the other town. I don't have time to gaze at the uniform for long because the first masked man runs at me. He doesn't waste a second, loading his gun while he speeds up. I immediately go to smack his head with the saucepan, but I miss, and he lunges for me. His mouth snarls and his eyes are red with hatred. He eventually lands on top of me and takes the weapon from my hand. His sleazy grin widens since I am now left defenceless. I don't know how long I can hold him off for with just my strength. He grips both my wrists using his strong hands and slams them against the floor. I cry out in pain as my side trembles beneath him. His bony knees dig straight into my bandage and the fire within me screams out for mercy. My whole body quivers in pain as droplets of sweat overcome me.

"Thought you were getting away, did we?" he spits. He has a firm grip as I try to squirm out of his clutch.

"You're going to pay for your little *friend*." His eyes are red pools of evil. I don't see any form of sanity left in them. I stop fighting against him and leave him slightly confused for a moment. Only a moment. When he stops wrestling with me, I quickly bring my knee up and kick him between his legs. His body falls to the floor beside me as the pressure against my side lightens.

"You bitch!" He cries out in pain, holding himself. I jump up from the floor, wincing, taking his gun and sword from his brown leather belt. He rolls around on the floor in pain and I slam the gun into the side of his head.

I catch my breath and see Dale struggling against the other two. The man with the knife has gotten off the floor and is headed towards Dale again. He runs with venom in his eyes and holds his knife out, ready to attack. *Oh no he doesn't!*

I hold my gun ready to shoot, gently pulling the trigger back, but I hear another loud bang as his body falls limp to the floor. I quickly turn around to see Troy and Zoe crouching down on the staircase. I smile at them and charge at the two men Dale's fighting off. Dale takes punch after punch. He isn't fazed while the men fight with everything in them. I run at them and slam the handle of the sword into the first guy's neck. He holds the back of his head in pain and mostly frustration, turning around to face me. I elbow him in the head, causing him to stagger backward. Dale stands, punching him once more, and his body falls lifelessly to the floor. When we turn around to face the last man, he hesitates and runs out the back door. I nod at Dale and he smiles back. After double-checking that each man is unconscious, we quickly run to the stairs toward Zoe and Troy.

"We need to go!" I shout. They both hand us our backpacks and black boots. A few seconds later, we are out the door and running miles from the house.

My side throbs and the pain has gotten a lot worse since we

fought those men back at the house. The sky has opened up and a light rain has started to fall. I wrap my jacket tight around me, savouring the last bit of heat I have left. Zoe holds my hand while we continue to walk, heading north. Her leg seems to have improved a lot and she can now walk by herself. She also tugs her jacket around her shivering body, fighting off the beads of icy rain. We are finally far enough away from the house that we have all started to relax a bit.

"Who were those men?" Zoe looks up at me, wiping away the heavy droplets of rain from her face. Her red hair is drenched and sticks to her purple cheeks. I hold her tightly next to me, ignoring the pain of my side in an effort to keep her warm.

"I don't know." I shake my head.

"I don't understand them." Dale starts to walk on the other side of me and Zoe. His shirt is completely soaked through, revealing his lower stomach muscles. The rain is starting to come down harder and the damp air sends a chill up my body.

"Who do you think they were?" I look at Dale, furrowing my brows.

He shrugs. *He knows just as much as I do.* Troy stays silent, walking ahead, keeping alert for danger. His shirt is also soaked through but it doesn't faze him. He still walks with strength and power, almost complete adrenaline.

"How did you get to that building in the first place, Zoe?" I ask, looking at her drenched little face.

The rain has soaked us all, but we find a few trees nearby and hide under the long branches. It seems to block out most of the rain but the cold air is just as bad.

"Those men grabbed me." Her little face looks up, meeting my gaze. She shivers in the cold wind.

"They grabbed you?" My eyes widen.

"Yeah, I went downstairs to get a drink out of our backpacks and they came in through the back door." Zoe starts to sniffle from the cold.

"She told us everything, Ella." Dale nods and so does Troy.

"So why were we still staying there if we were in danger?" *Am I the only sane one here?* Why would they stay there if those men could come back?

"Because you had just been *shot!* We didn't have anywhere else to go." Troy glares at me sternly.

"So they just grabbed you?" I raise my eyebrows at Zoe and she nods.

"They took me and said they would help me. I started to fight against them and he said once I go back with them, I could bring my friends too." She shakes her head. "They were lying and I knew it!" Zoe starts to cry. Small tears fall from her sparkling eyes as I hold her close. She wraps her ice-cold hands around me and I clench my eyes shut from the agony. The agony of mine and Zoe's pain.

"There was this little boy. They took us to a room and questioned us." She starts to shake.

"Hey, it's okay." I stroke her back, trying to keep her warm. She has gone through so much more than a nine-year-old should and it angers me. Almost to the point where I want to go stomping back to the factory.

"They shot him," she sobs into me.

"Why did they shoot him?" I ask, trying to keep her calm. She shrugs.

"He wasn't answering their questions properly."

"What do you mean?" I wipe away her tears and Dale leans in towards us, equally trying to keep Zoe warm from the cold.

Hailstones are now falling from the weeping sky above. They shatter against the branches of the forest we sit under as we watch the dreadful weather unfold before us.

"He kept answering things in a funny language," she sniffles again.

I give Dale a funny look and he furrows his brows, thinking.

"A funny language?"

Zoe looks at me and nods. Tears stream down her face as she remembers the awful scene.

"He kept saying things that didn't make any sense."

Dale pulls out his dry jacket from within his bag and wraps it around her.

"You'll freeze." I say, looking at him. He's just in a T-shirt.

"Zoe, tell Ella the rest." Dale does his best to comfort her, completely ignoring me.

The wind whistles past and the cold air bites into my side, pain shooting through me. I try to block it out, but every so often, I flinch from the slow torture. Troy studies me carefully, staying quiet.

"They shot him and I ran. I ran downstairs and hid. That's when you found me." She smiles weakly at that thought.

I'm so glad I found her in time or she could have got badly hurt. I hold her closer to me as we let the rain ease off.

"His body just lied there." Zoe looks to the floor.

None of us have spoken in a while, trying to process what's happened. We all look up when Zoe speaks.

"Hey, it's okay. You're safe now." I hold her hand and squeeze it. She nods but I know it's not something a nine-year-old should have to see.

"What do you think they want?" I ask Dale, who is staring off into the rain. He looks at me with a blank expression.

"I don't understand why they're shooting people, when there's not many of us left." He shrugs. *Why are they shooting people?* The same question whirls around in my head.

"The rain looks like it's keeping the zombies away though."

Dale half smiles.

Small droplets land on the ground around us but the branches still keep us sheltered from the harsh thunder of rain still falling from the sky.

"How's your side, Ella?" Troy's deep voice comes from my left as he sits holding his sword, digging it deep into the ground in frustration.

"It's fine," I say, avoiding the question. I don't want them worrying when it's not our biggest problem. Troy narrows his eyes at me. He knows I'm lying but stays quiet.

"How far away are we from The Society?" I ask.

Troy gets out the map from his pocket and we all sit around looking at it. "I'm guessing we are about here." He points to a spot halfway up the map.

"How long do you think it will take to get there?" I ask, looking up at his deep brown eyes. His hair is still damp from the rain and his clothes are completely soaked through still. I can't help but notice his rippling muscles through his drenched top, sticking deliciously to his skin. I quickly avert my eyes away.

"A few days, if we are lucky." Troy takes the map back as the rain starts to lighten a little.

"Do you think it's real?"

"The Society?" Troy answers, looking confused.

"Yeah."

He thinks it over for a moment and digs his sword further into the ground.

"I think it's our best hope. There must be something there. Why else would Derrick give us a map?" He raises an eyebrow.

"I don't know, but I hope it's there. We can't keep living like this." I gesture around and spot Zoe and Dale laughing a few feet away. They both stand up and Zoe has her hand out, trying to catch single droplets of rain. She giggles when they tickle her palm. Dale holds her hand out, laughing with her. I smile at the two of them. I'm so glad Zoe is feeling comfortable around Dale and Troy, just in case something did happen to me.

"I admire you, Ella." Troy says. I whip my head back around.

"You do?" I ask, not understanding.

"You really care for Zoe, don't you?" He smiles weakly and looks up at me.

"We are all she's got," I answer, looking back at the two of them. Zoe has brightened up since we've left the house behind.

"You're stronger than you think, Ella." Troy's dark expression meets mine and I smile.

"I have to be."

"No, you don't." He shakes his head and starts to stand. The rain has almost stopped falling now. "We should go, leave some distance between us and the town, just in case they follow." He helps me up from the damp ground and we grab our belongings. Dale and Zoe join us as we trudge over the wet, soggy ground.

The air is calm and damp and the cool breeze against my cheeks is quite refreshing. Troy and Dale walk ahead, and I walk alongside Zoe. We have started to relax a little as we walk miles north. My feet have started to throb for the last few hours, but I keep pushing on. We can't afford to stop. I admire Zoe's determination. Most nine-year-olds would be complaining the whole journey, but she stays silent, keeping a smile on her face. I start to hear a strange noise coming from behind us, so I take a deep breath and turn around. A mangled body runs towards us. White spots cover its pale skin but it runs at a super speed, gaining on us.

"Get Zoe out of here!" I shout. Dale immediately picks her up, running in the opposite direction.

Chapter 19

"ELLA!" ZOE SCREAMS, RUNNING AWAY from me and the rotting zombie.

Its mangled head is hanging off to the side, as if it's already been in a fight with someone else. A part of me hopes it is Kira, Mark, and George…but I know the chances are pretty low. Its eyes are distant but full of hunger. Raw bones snap in the monster's arms as they fall to the ground, each part of its decaying body slowly dying from the inside out. I grab my sword, holding my ground, and I stare at the zombie running towards me. Troy runs over and stands by my side, doing the exact same thing. When his dark expression meets mine, I know that he's ready to fight.

Is it a lone zombie, or are there others? It runs at us as green blood seeps out from its skin, from its pores, and any living flesh still hanging from its body. The monster is badly injured but that doesn't stop it. It comes closer and Troy quickly stabs it through the heart. He draws his sword back as the creature cries out and drops to the floor. It slowly starts to crawl towards my feet with a hungry expression. *How is it still alive?* I jump on its back, its bones crunching underneath my feet. It eventually stays down and doesn't move. We look around for more but can't see any. Suddenly we turn around and find Zoe running over to us.

"Zoe?" I run to her, meeting her halfway.

"It's Dale! He's hurt!" she shouts. Troy picks her up, but I'm already racing ahead to find Dale when Troy catches up, running alongside me.

"Where is he?" I ask, as we sprint. She points, and then we see it — a group of zombies surrounding a body lying on the ground.

"Dale!" I scream, running over to them. All the zombies snap their heads around. Their eyes look different. Demonic even. Something's off. Had the zombies planned this attack? I thought they weren't smart. I thought they couldn't communicate.

"The lone zombie was a freaking decoy!" I shout, running at the group of diseased monsters.

"Dale!" I scream again, sprinting over.

I grab my sword and slice the head off the first one as it falls to the floor, rolling away. The others look old but still as deadly. I stab the next one in the heart as a rotting hand grips around my leg. Another grabs my arm, digging in their gruesome chipped nails. I curse, shouting out, and stamp on the zombie's hand. I try to shrug off the other as a loud gunshot goes off. The hand lets go of my arm and green blood splatters from its pale white skin, landing on my face. *Ew*. I wipe away the green, infected blood and look around to see Troy standing with a gun pointed out, protecting me and Zoe. I continue to run over to the body lying on the ground.

"Dale?" I shout, a small tear trickling down my cheek. The cold air stings my skin and my blisters throb with every step on the ground.

The body comes into view, but it's not Dale. The body is of a boy with short blonde hair. His clothes are damp and dirty and his shoes are missing. The bottom of his trousers are torn and his body lies lifelessly on the ground.

"He's not dead," Dale's voice comes from behind me. His body is raked head-to-toe in cuts and slashes, his dark hair damp with sweat and his face covered in specks of dirt. His T-shirt has risen slightly, showing off the intense, tanned muscles lying beneath. I find myself suddenly lost for words.

"Dale?" I splutter. I surprise him by running over to hug him. I wrap my arms around his shoulders, a second trembling tear escaping my watering eyes. His strong arms embrace me as he takes a deep breath. I finally let go and look up to see Dale's cheeks slightly flushing red.

"I thought you were dead!" I hit him on the shoulder, but it doesn't seem to faze him in the slightest. He mockingly acts offended.

"You're not getting rid of me that easily." He winks slyly and I laugh.

Realising we are still on the verge of a zombie attack, we gather ourselves together and walk towards the body on the ground.

"He's just unconscious." Dale checks him over.

"Has he been bitten?" I ask, looking wary of the boy in front of us.

I really don't do well with strangers anymore, especially the innocent-looking ones. The boy has small freckles lining his cheeks, and his torso is weak and thin. He looks about the same age as Dale, which explains why I thought it was him from a distance.

"I don't think so," Dale answers.

Troy and Zoe run over. "What happened?" Troy asks, out of breath. His face too, equally covered in dirt and slashes. Dried blood stains his clenched jaw, sweat rolling down the sides of his face.

"Me and Zoe were surrounded — we didn't stand a chance. And when I told Zoe to get to safety, she ran to find you." Dale stands up, brushing off his trousers. "I tried to fend for myself but the zombies were too much. Then this guy came running in from nowhere and helped fight them off. A zombie knocked him unconscious on the floor and I killed the rest of the creatures with your help." Dale nods at me.

"You think it was a distraction, the lone zombie?" I ask. *Could zombies really be that smart?*

Troy and Dale think it over and Zoe grabs my hand, looking down at the boy's body.

"He's not going to die, is he?" Zoe's terrified eyes look up at me.

"No, I don't think so."

"I didn't think zombies were that smart," Troy says, shaking his head.

"Maybe they're a lot smarter than we give them credit for," Dale shrugs.

"We need to get out of here before more show up though." Troy puts his sword and gun away deep within his belt.

Dale listens for a heartbeat from the boy's chest. "He's definitely alive. Come on, help me carry him." Dale starts to stand, getting three blank stares in return.

"We're not taking him along, *are* we?" I ask, warily. I don't know whether I trust this boy — he could be a murderer or a rapist, and I'm not taking any chances. He could also be infected.

"He sacrificed his own life to help me, Ella. I'm not leaving him here to be eaten." Dale looks at me sternly.

"What if he's been bitten? He will turn into a zombie," I reply. Zoe grasps my hand tighter in fear from my words.

"I don't think he has," Dale says, standing firm.

"What do you think?" I look up at Troy and he seems to be

thinking it over.

"I don't see the harm of taking him along with us. If he starts to turn into a zombie, we will have to shoot him," Troy replies, looking blankly at the boy's body. I guess he has a point and I understand why Dale doesn't want to leave him here.

"Fine. But if he starts acting strange, then he's gone. Agreed?" I ask. Everyone nods their agreement, so I help Dale carry him. Troy offers Zoe a piggyback, giving her a much needed rest from walking. We take turns carrying his body for a few miles, but darkness starts to invade the sky as we head towards a river in front of us. We set his body down and set up camp for the night.

We open up a tin of food between us and keep an eye on the boy lying on the ground. We have propped his head on a backpack and left him to rest. None of us want to use the river to bathe in, just in case the water is infected. With all of our cuts and open blisters, we can't take the chance of infecting our blood with the disease.

"Do you think we can trust him?" I ask.

"I don't see why not," Troy says, looking at the boy behind me.

"He seems okay," Dale adds. Then he digs into his food.

"How's your side?" Troy asks. He furrows his brows slightly, silently assessing me. His hypnotic brown eyes latch onto my own when I meet his gaze. There's a darkness shadowing the sparkle of light. He's been through hell just like the rest of us, but just by one look I find myself blushing, my stomach nervously flipping over in frantic somersaults.

"To be honest, I haven't given it much thought," I reply, looking away. There's no way I can hold his gaze any longer without melting on the spot. *Focus, Ella! Get a grip!*

"Ella, you need to look after yourself a bit more," Dale says, raising his eyebrows at me. "Do you want me to take a look?"

"No, I'm fine."

"No, you're not. I'm going to take a look." He puts down his food and walks toward me.

I roll my eyes as we head over, away from Zoe and Troy. I don't really want Zoe or Troy to see how bad it is, since they worry about me enough. Dale carefully lifts my top up a little and undoes the bandage so he can look.

"God, Ella. This looks badly infected," he sighs, getting a good look at the raw flesh. "Um…Ella, I think we have a slight problem," he mumbles.

"What?" I ask, confused.

"Well, I don't know how to say this, but your open wound has been infected. The zombie blood has gotten inside your bandage." Dale's horrified expression tells me everything I need to know.

"But I don't understand…"

"It must have been when you fought those zombies earlier, when you thought that boy was me." Dale looks up at me and my eyes start to water.

"I'm going to die." I just state the true fact. I'm going to die painfully. "Just shoot me." My body trembles with my own words. The virus will spread through me, I know it will. I'll end up like my family, like every other helpless victim.

"What?" Dale's mouth gapes open.

"Just do it. I don't want to turn into a zombie. Just kill me now." The words break my heart. I've been fighting them off for so long and now I'm going to turn into one.

"But we don't know if you will, Ella. It's been a few hours and you haven't turned yet." He raises an eyebrow. His gentle fingers brush over the wound and I clench my eyes shut from the agonising pain. "You might get lucky."

"But what if I hurt you. I can't let myself hurt you, any of you." I crumble to the floor and Dale carefully sits next to me.

"You won't." He smiles weakly. He knows that I will turn, but he can't bring himself to kill me. He knows that it will happen, just like I do. It's only a matter of time now.

"Promise me, you'll shoot me when I start to act strange," I demand.

"Ella..."

"Promise me!" I shout.

He nods weakly, grabbing something from his bag.

"I will do my best to clean it out. Maybe it won't have infected your blood yet." He dabs a cold liquid onto the skin and I wince from the pain. My skin feels like it's on fire as it shoots through me.

"Try to relax a little." Dale tries his best to keep my writhing body still. I nod and clench my eyes shut. "I'm just cleaning it." Dale's soft voice is calming and I try to relax through the agony while he gently places the bandage back on.

"Do you carry all this stuff around with you?" I ask, raising an eyebrow as the pain starts to disappear.

"Yeah, I figured someone would need it at some point." He smiles up at me.

The pain of knowing I will have to leave this group hasn't hit me yet. I will have to leave them before the zombie inside me takes over. Before I hurt any of my friends. The thought of leaving Zoe rips through my chest. How on earth will I ever be able to leave her? But I quickly remember that I cannot care for her anymore. I will soon be a monster. The same monsters that I've been trying my best to destroy. I will soon be a murderer, the same murderers that killed my family. The anger blazes through me. *How could I have been so careless, so stupid to let myself get infected?* I shake my head and look up when I hear an unfamiliar voice.

"Ouch, that looks painful," a voice says, from behind Dale. We both look around to find the blonde-haired boy awake. He stands, looking down at us. I quickly drag my top down to cover myself up.

"Careful, Ella. Don't make it worse." Dale quickly wraps the bandage around my lower stomach and helps pull my top back down.

"Sorry. I'm Ethan." The boy smiles and holds out his hand. I'm wary to take it but Dale stands to take it instead.

"I'm Dale and this is Ella." He gestures toward me and Ethan smiles in my direction for a moment longer than necessary. I start to feel uncomfortable in my own skin as his eyes watch me.

"Nice to meet you." Ethan looks back at Dale.

"Are you okay? Do you need anything?" Dale studies him for injuries. *He's definitely got the doctor thing going for him.*

"Nah, I'm fine, man. Just a little bruise," Ethan replies, laughing. I just frown at him. He definitely seems too friendly and too relaxed to be here by himself.

Troy and Zoe walk over and Ethan introduces himself. Troy doesn't look impressed by this new guy either and Zoe seems very wary of him. I guess you can say we're not a very social group.

"So, where are you guys headed?" Ethan sits down next to us and I look at Troy, silently asking whether to let him know, just in case we can't trust him.

Troy narrows his eyes but Dale starts to speak. "We are headed north, to The Soc…"

"We are headed north!" I snap. They both stare at me, surprised by my little outburst. "Just north." I glare at Dale.

Dale finally gets the message and stays silent. I can almost see a slight grin on Ethan's face.

"She's a feisty one, huh?" Ethan smirks. "I like feisty." He winks at me.

I'm not even sure I heard the last bit of that sentence right, because he mumbled it so quietly that even a mouse wouldn't be able to hear.

"You will leave Ella alone!" Troy takes his eyes away from the sky and glares down at Ethan.

Troy could easily pick Ethan up by the shirt and toss him into the lake if he wanted — that's how much pure anger and strength he shows. I don't need protecting, but it's nice to know that he has my back.

"Chill man, only messing." Ethan smiles, but it doesn't reach his eyes.

I see something in them that instantly turns me against him. Something's off about him. Just the way he sits, the way he moves. He's definitely too relaxed and chilled out for a zombie survivor. I furrow my brows. I demand to know more about him, something to prove my theory. Zoe edges closer to me while she scans the stranger in front of her. Her eyes narrow every time he speaks, just like mine.

"So, where are you from?" I ask, trying to pry information from him. His Australian accent is a huge giveaway but I feel rude not to ask.

Troy turns to raise an eyebrow at me, as if puzzled by my question. I ignore him and focus on the lying rat in front of us. Okay, so maybe lying rat is too strong for someone I've only just met, but it is how I feel.

"I'm from Sydney originally but I came here on holiday," he replies, shaking his head. "Some holiday," he laughs, snorting at his own sarcasm.

Liar! My inner voice screams.

"Are you on your own?" Troy asks, interrupting my inquisition. I scowl at him and I think I see a small smile emit on his lips. Troy knows exactly what I'm up to and he wants to join in. *Jerk.* This is my inquisition, not the Ella and Troy show.

"Yeah, for a while now actually." Ethan shrugs and his gaze meets mine. "How about you? Ever visit the land down under?" He winks at me again and grins.

Uh oh. Troy immediately stands, not bothering to take any

more crap from him, and towers over Ethan. He holds him by the throat and I can see pure hatred in his eyes. Complete and utter venom for this new guy. The sight is quite entertaining for a few seconds, but I quickly try and douse the situation.

"Troy, it's okay." I walk over and try to pry his tight grip from Ethan.

"A little respect wouldn't go amiss," Troy growls at Ethan, only centimetres from his face. *He is seriously pissed.*

I don't need someone standing up for me, but he seems to have it under control now, so I let him continue.

"Look dude, chill. I was only joking." Ethan holds up his hands in defeat. I roll my eyes. *Boys.*

Troy looks him up and down and decides he isn't worth it and walks away. Ethan smirks at the thought of winding up Troy and when he turns around, Ethan grins at me again. I avert my eyes away from him, acting unmoved by his sleazy charm.

After we have finished eating, we all decide to get some rest. Me and Zoe sleep huddled up together with Troy and Dale a few feet away. Ethan sleeps about a hundred yards away under the order and watchful eye of Troy. If he was any further away from us, he would be on the other side of the lake. If Troy could, I think he'd have no problem throwing him in the river, into the infected water. I can't help but giggle a little at the thought, while imperceptibly shaking my head. Ethan is a problem. His attitude seems too relaxed and slightly strange for a lone survivor. If that's his true story, he could just be making it all up. He probably isn't here on holiday at all.

The dark sky looms over us all and the full moon beams down. I sigh, wondering how on earth I can sleep knowing Ethan is here with us. Even the sound of his name makes me shiver with uneasiness.

"Beautiful night," Ethan shouts, from where he lays a few hundred yards away. Troy turns away from him, muttering something under his breath.

I look up at the sky, glancing at each small, glistening star. The moment reminds me of my old life. Sitting with Leila on the porch swing, counting each individual star until we fall asleep. I used to hold her so close, so tight that no one could ever hurt her. A warm tear runs down my cheek and I shake it away, feeling stupid. I can't think about my old life now. It's over. Nothing is ever going to be the same again. As I look back across the dry landscape, I catch Ethan looking over at me. His whole demeanour makes me shiver. I narrow my eyes and sit up.

"I'll take first watch," I say, standing up, grabbing my sword, and sitting next to a tree trunk nearby.

A large woodland area surrounds us and keeps us dry in case the weather decides to rain again. The darkness within each tree and bush makes me feel very uneasy. Anything could strike at any moment. I stay aware, looking out into the night for any movement, any slight noise that interrupts the silence. I will not allow my friends to become infected like me. I will protect them with all that I have left, even if it means I won't rest until I'm dead. *I soon will be.* I shake the thought away. I look around at the others. Zoe has snuggled up next to Dale. Troy lays looking up into the stars, and I wonder what he's thinking about. How will he respond to me leaving? Another pain shoots through me. A pain that surprises me. I furrow my brows. *Do I have feelings for Troy? No, I can't have. How can I develop feelings for someone that I hardly know?* The slight glimmer of hope that latches onto every one of his steely gazes and his stubborn acts is growing with every second. I need to cut the hope down. I need to take control of my emotions. *What if he's the first person I want to kill as a monster?* The thought startles me.

After another hour of thinking irrationally, I decide not to think anymore. I focus all my energy on protecting what's left of this group. Silence answers me. The eerie wind whisking past my hair. I have a feeling this is going to be a very long night.

CHAPTER 20

AFTER A FEW HOURS, I start to drift off while staring into the dark woods, but immediately snap my eyes back open. I shake myself awake and keep watch. *Focus, Ella!*

"Hey," a soft voice comes from behind me. *What time is it?*

I look around to find Troy taking a seat next to me on the small rock. The moonlight highlights his dark features, his slight stubble growing against his strong jaw, and his ripped muscles that lie in wait under his shirt. As I watch him carefully, I see the small sparkle of hope in his hazel eyes that look out into the night.

"Hey," I reply.

I follow his gaze, spotting a few purple flowers blooming a couple feet away, and I smile. The small amount of life growing in this world is the only hope we have, and the thought that such small beauty still exists amongst all the horror fills me with warmth.

"Do you think things will ever go back to normal?" I ask, terrified of the answer. I know things will never be the same again, so why even ask? *Am I trying to reassure myself?* Troy knows the answer I'm looking for, but he can't bring himself to admit that the world is just going to get worse.

"No," he says, looking down at the floor and then back up at me. "But maybe it's the start of something new." His dark eyes take me in, his emotionless expression giving nothing away.

"Maybe this is a way of starting over."

Does he really think that? A way of starting fresh? It seems like more of a punishment. The world is filled with hungry demonic creatures that want to rip our hearts out, we've lost most of our families, we are struggling for supplies and shelter, and Troy thinks it's the start of something *new?* I lift my head back up, sighing. I guess he's trying to be positive, to highlight what could be in the future. I haven't given much thought to what's going to happen ahead of tomorrow, whether we'll all make it, whether we'll all survive…

"Yeah, I guess." I smile weakly at him and he holds my gaze.

"Here." He holds his hand out towards me.

A single purple flower sits in his palm. It's beyond beautiful in all its loneliness. The individual violet leaves glisten and light up the middle of the flower. Little beads of water still float in the tip and each petal glows with life, with hope. The same hope that grows within me. The same hope that craves for the touch of the boy sitting next to me.

"There's always something beautiful, you just have to look for it." Troy's words melt me from the inside out. Any doubt that I feel is washed away with just one look, all the horror and the loss suddenly feels worth it to sit by his side, to watch him move, to feel the electricity sparking rapidly between us.

I take the precious flower from his hand and meet his gaze once again. "Thank you." A small smile emits from my lips as I see a softer side in his expression.

"There are only a few precious things left in this world." His eyes grow darker and he holds a much more serious expression.

I can't think. My mind is like jelly. I cannot hold onto any rational thought as I get lost within his eyes, those eyes that hold the same torment as my own. He has a past just as deep as mine and he has scars that are etched onto his heart, but doesn't show them. I know that now. He doesn't let anyone in because he can't bear to lose anymore.

I bite my lip. His longing expression could have any girl at their feet in seconds. He gazes at me with an intensity that I've never seen before. His eyes quickly change to pure passion as he gently moves a strand of blonde hair away from my face. He softly tucks it behind my ear, caressing my skin with a fiery touch. My heartbeat starts to rapidly convulse and the butterflies I've been trying to murder flutter around violently in the pit of my stomach. The heat from his hand immediately sends electric currents throughout my body as a warm smile lights up his face.

"Not interrupting anything, am I?"

Troy quickly takes his hand away and I whip my head around to see Ethan smirking at us. *Great timing.* I look back at Troy and he glares at Ethan. *If he hadn't already pissed him off then this had to be the icing on the cake.*

"Sorry, guys. I didn't mean to ruin the moment." Ethan tries to look apologetic, but he couldn't look more amused with the situation.

"Sure you didn't," I hear Troy mumble under his breath, and I feel a protective arm slide its way, unbearably close to my skin, across the small of my back. A little possessive of Troy, but I don't mind in the slightest. I can't believe how much I crave his touch when his hand is lingering only inches away, even his arm behind my back sends my stomach in somersaults.

"Thought I'd take Ella's place and let her get some rest." Troy still glares at Ethan, almost warning him off me.

"I'd better get some sleep," I say, getting up and walking away from the situation. The close contact with Troy is suddenly broken and I immediately miss the heat flowing between us. I half smile at Troy as I walk over to where Zoe and Dale sleep.

Ethan grins at me as I walk past and it makes me feel uncomfortable yet again. What is it with him? Is it only me who feels this way about him? He's definitely too good to be true.

"I can be lookout, if ya want?" I hear Ethan say to Troy.

"You've got to be joking," Troy answers, shaking his head. I smile at his protectiveness of the group.

I settle myself down next to Dale and Zoe and the butterflies miraculously seemed to have calmed down a little, but some still flutter. I stare up at the twinkling stars in the sky and take one more look at the beautiful purple flower in my hand. Soon enough I find myself drifting off to sleep as the darkness overcomes me, dreaming of hazel eyes and steely gazes.

I wake up to a loud crash. I bolt upright, wincing from the pain in my side and check around for Zoe. She sits up next to me, her eyes just as wide as mine as we both wildly scan the area.

"We've gotta get out of here!" Troy shouts, running over to us. My blurry vision starts to disappear, shaking myself awake.

"What?" I ask, confused.

Dale immediately picks up Zoe and his backpack.

"Ethan is one of THEM!" Troy helps me up and grabs our belongings.

"One of who?" I ask, getting a better look at Troy. His face is covered in raw cuts, with blood seeping out the sides.

"Are you okay?" I ask, scanning him for more injuries. *Okay, stupid question, but I need to know what's going on.*

"I'm fine, but I need to get *you* out of here!" Troy grabs his sword.

"What's going on?" I ask, darting my eyes around for any potential threats, but I see nothing.

"I followed Ethan last night and left Dale in charge. I knew he was up to something. I saw him with those men carrying guns, wearing the green uniforms." He runs both his hands through this hair in exasperation. "They saw me and attacked. They're right behind me!" He grabs my arm and we start to run.

Dale carries Zoe and sprints alongside us.

"They're following us?" I ask. Troy just nods.

We run wildly through the trees of the woodland, passing hundreds of brown leaves and jagged branches, each one ripping at my clothes that much more. The morning air is crisp and damp as the wind hits my cold cheeks. I lose my balance when I slip up on the mud beneath my feet and my hands land in the soggy wet ground. Troy helps me up.

"Ella, come on!" He grabs my hand, lifting me out of the dirt, and we run as fast as we can through the woods. Suddenly gunshots go off behind us.

"Ethan is one of them?" I ask, as we run.

"Yeah, I knew we couldn't trust him!" Troy shakes his head while we sprint forwards faster and faster, following Dale and Zoe.

"What do they want?" I ask, shouting.

To kill you! To rip you apart! My inner voice snarls at me.

"Us dead, I presume," Troy yells through the chaos.

Suddenly something lunges for me and jumps out of the line of trees. I come face to face with a diseased zombie and it claws at my throat. I scream when it hits my side. We both go flying to the ground, but Troy drags it off me with his strong arms, stabbing it in the heart. My eyes are wide in horror as I bring my hand to my throat. Another few gunshots go off nearby while I try to stand in the mud. I look down at my hands that are now covered with red blood. The pain rips through me as I stagger to my feet.

"Go!" Troy yells as another zombie runs at him. "I'll hold them off!"

"No!" I scream, the agony of my throat ripping through me once again.

"Ella, go! We need to split up, *now*!" Troy glares at me, his whole body strong and courageous. His jaw clenches when he hears more gunshots, his eyes flickering between me and the people chasing us.

"I can't just leave you!" I yell, tears streaming down my face as blood pours from my neck. Troy walks over to me, carrying his sword and gun. His body moves with such ease and pure strength, his torso ripped with muscles, and I cannot take my eyes away from him.

"We need to split up. He knows I won't leave you, and he will follow me to get to you. You'll be safe with Dale. He'll protect you." His deep eyes take me in while he comes closer, and I can almost feel the heat from his body alighting my own. The same sparks fly between us yet again. The pain starts to subside as I get lost in those brown eyes that instantly relax me, that take me into a whole other world.

"But…" I start.

He takes his hand and touches my ice-cold cheek. The same electric currents flows through me as his perfect lips find mine. A sudden glow of warmth fills my body when I wrap my arms around his shoulders. This is what I've been craving. *Yes, yes, more.* He pulls me close and I feel his passion as he holds his other hand to the back of my neck. *Oh, yes!* His kiss is deep and passionate, like nothing I've ever felt before. The lust heating my body from the inside out as I lose all control. *More. MORE!* We get lost in each other's embrace. He pulls away when we hear a growl from a zombie behind us. *Hungry. SO HUNGRY!* A voice in my head startles me. *No! This can't be happening now!* Troy's kiss leaves me longing for more, longing for his touch, but I quickly shake away my inner-zombie thoughts and run off in the opposite direction, following his instructions. He watches me run away, not wanting to let me go. I need to go before I hurt him. *MUST TASTE.*

Where are Dale and Zoe? I can't hurt them either. I run faster over the muddy ground and hear low growls from behind me. I look around to see Troy fighting off three zombies. I want to run and help but I can't trust myself around him. The voice in my head is getting stronger and I can't control my actions. I continue to run through the trees, trying to get as far away from the others as possible. It's happening, I'm turning into a monster!

HUNGRY! SO HUNGRY! my inner-zombie roars.

Suddenly, an arm wraps its way around me and I stumble backwards. A rough hand covers my mouth tightly and I get dragged into the shadows of the trees. I try to scream, but it's no use. I get pushed against a wooden trunk, the bark stabbing my skin as my hands are held firmly against my back.

"Not so strong without your boyfriend around, huh?" the snarl spits into my ear.

The voice comes from behind me and I turn to see my attacker. Ethan's evil grin comes into view and I try to scream out again. His hand is held firm over my mouth and I feel his hot breath on my injured neck.

"If you do what I say, I won't kill you," he whispers in my ear seductively.

Taste. Must taste. Smells so good. My inner-zombie voice starts to get excited.

I shiver from his slimy well-being. His hand starts to grope my body and I try to fight him off. Beads of sweat cover me, fighting with all I have.

Bite him! Taste him! the zombie-Ella spurs me on.

"Get off!" I scream, biting his hand.

"You bitch!" he yells. But Ethan only tightens his grip on my wrists, pulling them hard against my back. I struggle in pain as he holds me against the tree.

"Feisty little thing, aren't you?" he laughs. His other hand explores my body freely, and I try to kick him but he stands strong, holding me in place. A tear escapes down my cheek. My throat hurts too much to scream, only a whisper leaving my lungs. I can't fight him off on my own. I'm not strong enough. His grotesque hand moves across my stomach and I wince as he hits my wound. He ties my arms in place, causing me to struggle against him.

"Now I know why Troy was so protective of you," he smirks. "He wouldn't let anyone else have you. You were off limits. Forbidden." He smiles wickedly and I try to scream out again. "Now you're all mine," he laughs, continuing to explore my body.

Tears escape down my face as I try with everything in me to fight him off. The zombie within me has gone for now. The voice has stopped. Fear has taken over and beaten the monster to the ground.

Ethan's fingers grip the waistband of my trousers and start to pull downward, but suddenly his hand lets me go. I look up to see Troy standing over him as Ethan lies on the ground, looking up in horror. Troy holds out his gun and holds it against Ethan's head.

"Don't *EVER* touch her!" he growls, pure animalistic murder in his eyes.

"Look, mate, I was only protecting her from the zombies, I swear." Ethan looks up at him, pleading.

Troy's eyes flicker with anger as he presses the gun harder against him.

"Do you hear me? Don't *EVER* touch her again!" Troy holds him down to the floor and Ethan swallows in fear.

In a sudden flash, Ethan grabs a knife out of his pocket and attempts to stab Troy. Troy grabs Ethan's wrist and smashes the handle of the gun against his head. Ethan lays unconscious on the floor as Troy comes over to me with a worried expression.

"Are you, alright?" His eyes scan me over.

I start to see a sudden movement coming from behind him as Ethan runs at Troy with a knife. Blood drips down his face where Troy hit him, his eyes now burning with rage.

"Troy!" I shout. He turns around to see Ethan coming for him.

Suddenly, a loud gunshot goes off as Ethan's body falls to the floor. I look up wide-eyed to see Troy holding a gun out in front of him. I look around to see Dale, with Zoe standing by his side. They hide in the trees a few feet away.

"Jesus, Ella! Are you okay?" Dale runs over to us with Zoe at his heels.

I look down at Ethan's dead body and I wipe away my hot tears. Troy hits the bark of a tree with his fist, shouting out, and grits his teeth in anger.

"I'm fine." I half smile at Troy and walk over to Zoe, crouching down to her level.

"Let's get you somewhere safe," I say, smiling at her. She hugs me back tightly.

"Ella, you're so brave." I feel her tears as she grips onto me tightly.

"Thank you," I sigh.

Dale smiles down at us. I look up and see Troy's expression, looking at me with guilt written all over his face.

"You didn't know he was going to do that," I say, walking over to him.

"I should have known." He shakes his head in disgust and adjusts his backpack.

"Are you sure you're okay?" Dale asks, scanning me over, his eyes immediately going to my side.

"I'm fine. Can we just get out of here please?" I take Zoe's hand

and look over to Troy.

"Thank you," I say, smiling at him. He nods at me.

"That bastard deserved it," Troy replies.

We walk away, hiding in the trees just in case we come across any other zombies or madmen nearby. My side hurts like hell, but we can't afford to stop. Every single fibre of energy I have left goes toward blocking out the pain, blocking out the agony that stings with every step. My flesh isn't just raw, it feels like pure ice. Ice that has frozen my whole stomach to a point where I'm throwing up every half an hour. The blisters layering on my feet are huge and I've never felt anything like them before. If the others are experiencing the same pain as me, they don't show it. *Just one more day and we should be at The Society.* I continually repeat the sentence over and over, hoping the words will calm me. I haven't really thought about what's going to happen when we actually get there. Is it even going to be there or has this just been some wild-goose chase?

A weak part of me hopes that my parents are still alive, but a strong part of me knows the disappointing truth. If they are still alive, then maybe I never knew them at all. *Maybe Derrick was lying about everything and there is no Society at all?* That thought whirls around in my head for a while. *If Derrick is lying and there is no Society, then why would he send us all the way out here? Unless something else is waiting for us?* I shake my head at the questions invading my mind and focus on what's important at this very moment. We will just have to deal with whatever awaits us when we get there. We need to survive for another day or so first.

I hope that Zombie Ella doesn't return, or else I will have to leave. I will have to get as far away from my friends as possible. I don't want to do that, if I don't have to. The zombie has only tried to take over once, but my fear is what had fought it off. I furrow my brows. Fear seems to be what zombies feed on, so why on earth did my own fear fight off the zombie inside of me?

I eventually look around at the group. Dale walks across the deserted road, his shoulders tense, and I can tell he's thinking about something. His shirt is torn in places and his boots are the muddiest I've ever seen them. Dale carries Zoe on his back, her head resting upon his shoulder. Zoe looks exhausted — her red hair is matted and her clothes are ripped to shreds. Troy walks alongside me, wearing the same leather clothes and a dull green shirt. As we trek out of the woods, we leave behind the carnage of our travels. Troy and Dale keep asking whether I'm okay every two minutes, but I assure them that no harm has come to me.

After a few more miles, my side screams with helplessness. Plain land now surrounds us. The sun beams down and the dusty earth beneath our feet is beginning to get easier to walk on. We continue to head north, sweating under the midday sun. Carrying a dozen backpacks doesn't help and we are running out of supplies too. We only have one more bottle of water left between us. As the scorching heat beats down we are finding it hard to keep up the pace. We all start to slow down, trying to deal with the heat. Every one of us is drenched in sweat as Dale eventually gets out the last water bottle and takes a sip. He hands it to Zoe and Troy and then offers me some.

"I'm alright," I say. He puts it in his backpack. The more water we save the better.

Others need it more than me, especially if I'm going to turn into a monster, and to be honest, I'm not that thirsty. We continue on for a few miles before taking a break. We all settle down on the rocky ground. I haven't seen a zombie around for miles but that doesn't mean we won't be surprise attacked. The zombies are smarter than we give them credit for and they are quite capable of ripping us all to shreds, given half the chance.

"How long have we got to go?" Dale asks. Troy gets out the map from his pocket, pointing to a spot, and we quickly try and guess our location. It doesn't look that far away from here but still quite a journey on foot. Zoe takes off her shoes and I see red blotches on her white socks that are now stained with dirt and blood. She takes off her socks, wincing from the pain of her blisters.

"Here." I hand her the cream I found in the old house and gently rub it on her feet. She keeps a brave face as I continue to rub in the cream. Every now and again she winces when the pain gets too much. She really is a brave little girl.

"Okay, now the other one." I put her white sock back on, careful not to make her feet any worse. She hands me her other foot and I continue to help her blistered feet.

"How's your side?" Troy asks.

"It's okay," I lie. I am good at blocking out pain, but it throbs harshly, and it isn't getting any better. I can feel it rubbing against the bandage, but I don't complain.

"Can I have a look?" Dale asks. I nod my consent.

I finish Zoe's feet and she thanks me. I walk over to Dale and he lifts up the bottom of my top, high enough to undo the bandage.

"You need to get someone professional to look at this," Dale says, looking at me warily.

"And where are we going to find someone like that in this nightmare of a world?" I ask sarcastically.

"It's getting worse." His worried expression drills into me.

"It's fine. I'll get it looked at when we reach The Society," I insist, brushing him off while he attempts to clean it. I sit as still as possible, blocking out the agony.

My side burns every time Dale touches it. Trying to keep still is like trying to keep my hand on a hot iron, but if it's going to help,

I can put up with it. I just hope The Society actually exists. Dale pops my bandage back over my wound, pulling my top back down.

"Thank you." I smile at him weakly.

"Seriously, Ella. Don't ignore that. Tell me if it gets too painful." He waits for me to argue, but I just nod. "Your neck doesn't look too bad now, so I'll just put some antiseptic on it to stop it from getting infected. I'll also put a plaster over it too." Dale begins attending to my neck. Once he's finished, I thank him again and look at Troy, who is watching me carefully with a blank expression.

"I think we should keep going," he says. Then he stands and helps me to my feet. "We can't waste any more time."

He helps Zoe onto his back, giving Dale a break, and we all gather up our belongings once again. I have taken off most of my layers, leaving me with just a black leather top and trousers. I pull my blonde hair back into a ponytail and pick up my backpack. We start to hear growling in the distance and start to walk a little faster, putting as much distance as we can between us and the zombies that linger behind, probably following the smell of fresh meat. I don't know how much of a fight we can put up at this moment. We are all exhausted and injured in some way. We're a walking meal to those creatures. Suddenly, I start to see smoke up ahead and I squint my eyes, trying to see where it's coming from. Maybe I'm just hallucinating.

"Can you guys see that?" I ask. They both nod.

Zoe looks up and narrows her eyes at the smoke rising into the air. It only looks a few miles away.

"Should we head towards it, or away from it?" Dale asks.

"I say we head towards it. Zombies shouldn't know how to make fire, so it may be other survivors," I answer.

"What if it's not? What if it's more madmen trying to kill all humanity?" Troy raises an eyebrow at me and I nod in agreement.

"I say we take the chance. It's north anyway. We can always go around if it looks too dangerous," Dale suggests, shrugging. We all agree to head towards the smoke.

Any sign of danger and we can all easily escape. We continue to walk for miles, the smoke getting closer and closer. The smell of food travels through the air and it speeds us up as our own stomachs grumble. I hear laughter. Familiar laughter up ahead. We trudge up the hill in front of us and when we finally get to the top, we see a two shadowed figures a few yards away. A fire flares up and the smell of food grows stronger. We make our way slowly towards the smoke of the fire.

"They don't sound dangerous," Dale says. I nod in agreement. As we get closer, I hear familiar voices.

The two figures come into view as we walk towards them. I see a rough shadow of a girl with long brown hair and tattered clothing. A much taller guy sits next to her and they are laughing together, holding hands. Zoe becomes wary of the strangers up ahead, probably because of what happened with Ethan. That's definitely going to give the group trust issues with strangers from now on.

"Ella?" a familiar female voice shouts, from where the two figures sit. The girl starts running towards me and I grab the handle of my sword, just in case.

Troy looks hesitant to carry on when the two figures start running over to us. The girl's face comes into view and I recognise her immediately.

"Kira?" I ask, my throat dry as she runs and wraps her arms around me.

"I can't believe you're still alive!" She squeezes me tightly and I laugh, not caring in the slightest about the pain from my side. "Not that you can't handle yourself, of course." She punches my arm and winks.

Another figure walks over to us and I smile as Mark comes

into view.

"You made it!" He beams a smile at us and Dale gives him a manly hug.

"I thought we lost you, man," Dale says, smiling.

"Nah, we got out of there alright," Mark laughs. They share a moment of male bonding. Friends reunited.

"How did you get here?" I ask.

"We headed north, just like we were going to, before we got split up." Kira leads us over to the fire and they both share their rations of food with us.

"I'm so sorry we left you, I didn't want to but…"

Kira interrupts me mid-sentence. "I completely understand why you did it. I would've done the exact same thing, given the situation. There was nothing you could've done. It would've been a death trap if you stayed." Kira smiles reassuringly at me and I feel a slight weight being lifted from my shoulders. "I guess you're wondering where the others are, huh?" Kira sits down next to me and Zoe. Zoe looks uneasy with the amount of people, so I keep her close to my side.

"Well, we ran into Jim." Troy smiles sympathetically, digging into his food.

"Yeah, we were ambushed. We weren't all going to survive." Kira shakes her head at the memory.

"How did you get out of town?" I ask, intrigued.

"Well, we started hearing zombies and waited as long as we could for you all to come back. George and Jim found an extra can of fuel in a compartment of the boot while searching around the truck," Kira smiles.

Mark continues the recalled story. "We quickly filled up the truck and the zombies started to attack, so we had to leave you guys behind. We drove the truck a few miles before we stopped to sleep, and while we were sleeping, we were attacked." Mark looks down at the ground.

"What?" I ask, open-mouthed.

"Yeah, Jim didn't stand a chance. We tried to climb out of the truck, but the zombies pushed it onto its side. George and I had just gotten Kira out in time when the zombies started to surround us. We tried to fight them off, but they were too strong, and they grabbed Jim by his throat. He had no chance." Mark sighs.

"So you travelled up here by yourselves?" I ask.

"Yeah, but we did run into a few bad, let's say, situations." Kira cocks her head from side to side.

We put out the fire while we finish off our food.

"What situations?" I look up at her and she carries on.

"We ran into these crazy men with guns and that's when we lost George. They started shooting at us when we were running away. George dove in front of me and a bullet hit him in the chest. He saved me." Kira looks down at the floor.

"Why did they try and shoot you?"

"We have no idea." They both shrug.

"We ran into them. They kidnapped Zoe, nearly killed Ella twice, and they stabbed Dale in the arm," Troy says. He looks up at Kira and Mark, both sitting there with their mouths gaping open, clearly at a loss for words.

"Wow, you've had a rough trip," Mark finally says, closing his mouth.

"Jesus, Ella. What happened?" Kira asks, noticing my blood-soaked top.

"I, um… got shot." I shrug and Dale narrows his eyes at me.

"She was in a lot of pain," he adds.

"You got shot?" Kira asks, mouth hanging open even wider.

"Yeah." I show her my bandage.

"Now I feel like a wimp for whining about my leg," Mark says, laughing.

"How is your leg?" Dale asks Mark.

"Yeah, it's alright. It's gotten better," Mark says. He smiles.

"I'm so glad you found us!" Kira beams at us, not quite believing we are back together as a group.

"We thought we'd never see you all again," she says, looking at the ground. Zoe huddles up next to me and I put an arm around her.

CHAPTER 21

ONCE WE FINISH RESTING, WE carry on north as a group. Daylight starts to slip away as the dark night takes over. The cool air against my skin is a relief from the blazing heat. Having Kira and Mark back has lifted our spirits — it's clearly on everyone's face. We are just about to setup camp for the night, until we spot a light in the distance. A small yellow light. We all look at each other in confusion.

"What the hell is that?" Mark asks, squinting into the darkness. The harsh yellow glow can be seen from miles away.

"Is that what I think it is?" I ask, looking over to Troy, but he doesn't look sure.

"There's only one way to find out," Kira winks at me.

"What if it's not?" I ask, suddenly feeling nervous. What if The Society doesn't exist and there's something awful waiting for us instead?

"Ella, you've come this far. Don't tell me you've chickened out on the last stretch?" Mark says. I immediately want to slap the grin off his face.

Troy glares at him for me, and I can't help but like his protectiveness.

"Fine, let's go." I gather up my belongings and pull on my backpack. Everyone follows my lead as I start walking towards the yellow light. "We should be there soon, everyone keep walking," I announce to the group, and everyone follows behind. *Since when did I become the leader?*

Nothing is going to stop me from getting some answers, from finding out the cause of this virus. Even if The Society doesn't help, I will have to dig for the truth. I will continue to fight in this world until I know what's happening and who those men are. I need to know what's going on, even if no one else does. I demand to know and I will find what I'm looking for.

As we cover more ground, I start to see a tall iron gate greeting us. The closer we get, the taller it looks. A small spotlight hangs off of the shiny metal wall, the yellow light streaming from its centre. It's about a hundred feet tall and we all look up in awe. We walk around to the front of the gate and see a soldier standing outside the main entrance. He is dressed from head-to-toe in black, his body covered in bullets and dark tattoos. His strong frame holds a large machine gun against his chest, ready to attack.

"Maybe he's friendly?" Kira snorts. We all narrow our eyes at her and it makes her grin even more.

"Maybe not," Troy replies curtly.

"Hey, lighten up," Kira laughs.

"I don't think now's the time to *lighten up*," Troy says, cutting Kira a hard look.

We reach the edge of the wall and start to move slowly towards the soldier. *Is this it? The Society?* I notice a yellow "S" painted on the outside of the metal wall. *Where have I seen that before?* I gasp, causing the guard to quickly snap his head around at us. He aims his gun out straight at me and marches over.

"Who are you?" the soldier demands, raising his head. He has short brown hair and quite attractive features. His expression is hard and fixated on me.

"I could ask you the same thing," I reply, stepping forward. He doesn't scare me.

"Don't get smart with me, miss." He holds his gun higher.

"My name's Ella," I say.

Dale and Troy walk over and stand by my side, with Zoe on Dale's back. Kira and Mark join us as well.

"More survivors, huh?" The solider narrows his eyes at the rest of the group.

"Yes, what is this place?" Kira asks.

"None of your business," the guard spits.

Kira bundles up her sleeves with her fists, cracking her neck to the side. She starts to march toward the guard, but Mark brings her back, securing her against him.

"Get off!" she shouts, fury blazing in her eyes at this cocky guard.

"No can do, babe," Mark says, rolling his eyes.

"You'd better keep your women in line." The guard's mouth curves up into a wicked smile. He's really getting on my last nerve. We didn't travel all this way to get treated like this.

I let out an angry snarl and start marching towards him, quite angry myself. Kira starts clapping her hands in excitement, still being tightly secured by Mark. Troy and Dale both quickly grab my arms and pull me back towards them.

"Ella, now's not the time," Troy whispers.

"Listen, we need to get to The Society. Do you know where that is?" Dale asks, raising an eyebrow.

"You'd better come with me." He gestures for us to follow and

I shrug at the others.

"Can we trust him?" Mark whispers. But no one answers as we follow the guard.

Troy's hand stays on his sword and Zoe has palmed a knife. *Seriously, where does she find them?* I'm totally blown away by this nine-year-old. Kira rolls her eyes as Mark still holds her close to him, as if he thinks she's going to go crazy and attack the guard at any given moment.

"What did you say your name was?" the guard asks, from over his shoulder. *I'm guessing he's talking to me.*

"Ella Holbert," I answer.

He doesn't reply but just nods instead, stopping at the gate in front of him. The wall stands tall with huge iron bars guarding the door. This place is well protected from zombies. Nothing could get past this wall.

"We have some new survivors. A Miss Ella Holbert and her friends," the soldier snarls. He is speaking into a little black radio on his shoulder.

The bars suddenly open and the sound causes me to jump. The guard smiles at me with a glint in his eye. *What is his problem?* The gate opens and we all warily walk through. The dark corridor is lit by small candles, and a few white cameras on the wall above us. Eventually we come to a stop before a dead-end. The wall lights up slowly, showing a buzzing screen. Green writing is displayed before us: **Discard Weapons Here.**

Suddenly a large drawer opens up in the wall and we all look at one another.

"I guess it's only fair since we won't be needing them to fend off zombies any longer," Dale says. He sighs and places his weapons in the metal drawer. Troy follows his lead, as do Kira and Mark. Zoe looks wary and eventually gives in too. She reaches down and pulls out four knives from her shoes and socks, five knives from within her pockets, and a small kitchen knife from behind her ear. Everyone turns to look at her with unreadable expressions. I can't help but look proud. She's a real fighter.

Once I've said goodbye to my sword and weapons, we walk through a detector. The machine scans us to make sure we carry no other weapons. Once we all make it though, we come to a stop before a large grey door in front of us.

"God, what's next? They'll want us to burn all our clothes and strip naked, most probably."

Kira starts pacing back and forth. Mark starts chuckling. "I don't know about you babe, but we've already…" he begins.

"Shut it!" Kira interrupts, punching Mark in the arm while he scowls at her.

Troy makes a grumbling noise which silences them both. Kira doesn't look happy and neither does Zoe. She stands by my side, grabbing for my hand. The grey door opens with ease, a dark room now standing before us. We all huddle up next to each other, preparing for what's next. *What is this place?* The lights snap on above me, bright white lights that immediately blind us. Troy squints his eyes, as do I, searching around for any other threats nearby. But as I look up, I'm met with a view that surprises me. Surrounding us are machines, machines that stand extremely tall. Each one sparks electricity while the white light acts as bars around the outside. The room is filled with them. As they turn on, coloured buttons light up on the sides and a green smoke comes from a grey machine on our left, highlighting a narrow tube in the middle.

"Welcome." A woman walks toward us. She has delicate, white-blonde hair that's pulled back into a tight bun. She wears a neat green uniform and holds a clipboard out in front of her. I immediately eye the small '*S*' tattoo on her neck. It's hidden underneath her collar with the top slightly showing.

"If you would like to step into the machine…" She continues

to graciously walk over to us.

"What are those machines?" I take a deep breath and the woman stops a few feet away from us.

"How rude of me. My name is Helen, and these machines determine if you have been infected by the virus. If you have, there is no use for you here." She smiles and it makes me feel uncomfortable.

A couple of guards stand in front of a large white door on our right, and a couple stand in front of another on our left. *No way out. Great.*

"Are you ready? It's only a quick process. You will be out of here in no time." Helen smiles again and writes something down on her clipboard.

"How do they work?" Kira raises an eyebrow and that makes Helen purse her lips. Obviously she hasn't had to argue with many survivors before.

"The machine scans your body effortlessly, searching for the drug that infects the human body. The same drug causing the monsters about to end humanity. We want to create civilisation again, but without any traces of the virus. You must pass this test or we will have no choice but to dispose of you." Helen looks emotionless.

Dispose? I gulp, knowing that my injury has been infected. Dale just looks at me in horror and I have to avert my eyes away.

"I'll go first." Troy steps in front of me and follows Helen to the machine.

He steps into the grey tube and she shuts a glass door around him. Helen starts to talk to Troy, but I can't hear what she's saying. Troy closes his eyes and the lights turn out around us. The whole room goes black and Zoe grips my hand tighter, standing as close to me as she can. The group huddles together while we all watch the machine light up neon-blue around Troy. After a few seconds, the lights come back on and Helen lets him out of the machine.

"Well done, Troy. Next please." Helen stands stoically as Kira walks over.

Each of us takes it in turns until the only ones left is just Zoe and me. The machine seems harmless and I guess they just want to make sure that we won't suddenly attack them.

"It's fine, Zoe. They are just checking you over for bites," I say, leading her over.

The others stand on the right side of the room by the grey door, waiting for us.

"Ella, I'm scared." Zoe looks up at me.

"It's alright. Just a little tickle, that's all." Helen starts to set up the machine for her.

"Hey, it's okay. I'll be here the whole time," I say to Zoe.

She nods, let's go of my hand, and steps into the machine. I stand just outside to make her feel more comfortable. The same thing happens again as the lights go out and Zoe closes her eyes. After a few seconds, the lights come back on and Zoe steps out of the machine.

"Wasn't that bad, was it?" I ask.

"No, it tickled." Zoe giggles and I give her a hug before she runs over to the others.

"I'll join you in a minute," I say. Zoe just nods. I sigh, knowing that I won't be joining them. I know that I've been infected. They'll know straight away. They will see my injury and my blood. They will see how badly injured I am and *dispose* of me.

"Ready?" Helen smiles at me.

No, I'm not ready. This is it. This is how my life is going to end. They will kill me, I know they will. They will shoot me in front of my friends, in front of Zoe. Maybe they'll take me somewhere else, to spare them the pain of watching me die. I can't handle what's about to happen. *Come on, Ella.*

"Fine." I step towards her. I look over to Dale and he looks away, thinking the same thing. He knows what's going to happen, so he takes Zoe's hand in his and squeezes tight.

"Fantastic." She smiles and leads me into the tube. I step into the cold metal and place my arms on the red crosses. Helen gently closes the glass in front of me. I stare out of it, with my heart beating furiously. Dale and Troy both wear the same worried expression, so I look away.

"What's your name?" Helen asks.

"Ella," I reply.

She smiles at me, with her perfect white teeth. "Right, Ella. Just close your eyes and this will be over as soon as possible." She gives me a reassuring look as I close my eyes.

The lights go out around me and suddenly my head goes blank. Darkness fills my mind as the machine sucks my memories from me.

Suddenly I find myself back in my hometown, my old house surrounding me. The cream-coloured walls. Both my parents stand in the kitchen. They whisper to each other. My sister runs at me and bounces on my lap, laughing. I laugh back as Henry sits next to me on the sofa. My parents join us in the front room, carrying dinner, and place it on the table in the middle of the room.

They smile at us. I'm suddenly transported to another time and place.

I sit in the backseat of the car. My mum and dad both stand outside, talking to a man with a hood up. The street is dark and the streetlamps glisten down on the shadows that surround them. The glow of the yellow light highlights a dark scar on the man's face. I must be young because I sit in the baby seat. As I stare out of the window, my parents hand an envelope to the hooded man. He nods, walking away. My parents walk back over to the car and start up the engine.

My head whirls around as I find myself spinning through a dark tunnel into my forgotten memories.

The rain pours down around me while I sit on the porch outside our house. My dad walks up the drive, returning home from work. I sit on an old wicker chair, smiling. Putting down my book, I run over to him. He holds out his arms and hugs me as I welcome him home. The rain drenches us and I look down to see a yellow S on his briefcase. I'm just about to comment when Leila and Mum walk out to greet Dad.

The memories are sucked from my mind. They remind me of things I don't want to remember — like the zombie attack on my town, losing Leila, and Henry. I start to think back over things. *Was I just naive? Did my parents know something?* More and more memories appear from nowhere, silently haunting me.

Me, Leila, and Henry run around the house shooting each other playfully — one of our many games. We are only little as we run into the basement.

"Can't catch me!" I shout, giggling.

"I'm going to get you, Ella!" Henry runs after me and Leila giggles, holding a fake gun.

I run away, down the basement stairs, and turn on the lights. Henry and Leila's soft footsteps can be heard behind me. I run and hide behind some tall shelving in the dusty part of the room. Cobwebs and old tools sit scattered around the dark, stuffy corner.

"You can't hide forever!" Henry says, laughing and crouching down like he's seen in movies. He holds out his fake gun and searches the room.

"Ella?" Leila runs behind him, almost knocking him over and

giggling.

I quickly jump out of my hiding place and pretend to shoot Henry. He drops to the floor and plays dead. Laughing, I grab Leila's hand and we run towards the stairs. Leila trips and falls on our escape from Henry.

"Ouch!" She holds her leg and I look down at what she's tripped on.

The grey stick is standing up out of the floor and as we look around at a loud sound, the basement wall starts to open up before us. Henry joins us and we stand there with our mouths gaping open.

"Good work, Secret Agent Leila!" Henry winks and walks into the room in front of us.

The walls have a big yellow S painted on them and I suddenly hear footsteps coming down the stairs.

"What are you kids doing?" Dad's voice booms from behind us and we all freeze, turning around slowly.

Leila skips over towards him and he picks her up. "We are secret agents!" She giggles.

Dad raises his eyebrows at me and Henry, and instantly we know we have done something wrong. "You're not allowed down here." Dad narrows his eyes at us in anger.

"Sorry, Dad." Henry hangs his head and walks back up the stairs, with me following behind.

Soon after that, our favourite playroom was taken away. Dad put a lock on the basement door and we were not allowed down there anymore.

Chapter 22

MY MIND SWIRLS THROUGH A dark cloud of fog once again and my body feels weak. I ache all over. I snap my eyes open to find Helen's worried expression staring back at me. I still stand in the tube of the narrow machine. She holds a black radio to her perfectly shaped lips and whispers some strange language into it. *What's she saying?* I try to listen but I can't make any of it out. Suddenly two guards grab me out of the machine and drag me to the left side of the room.

"Ella!" Zoe calls, already starting to run over to me.

A few more guards have run into the room, securing all my friends so they can't move. Zoe still runs towards me, the thought of being separated too horrifying.

"No! Ella!" she cries. But a guard catches her waist and drags her back to the others.

"Zoe!" I scream, the two guards already dragging me towards the little white door.

Troy tries to fight off the guards but more and more come in, holding him from running after me. His expression is filled with worry and absolute murder as he struggles his hardest to get to me. The two guards continue to drag me off into the doorway. The last thing I see are Zoe's watering brown eyes and the pain etched across her tortured face.

"Where are you taking me?" I demand, squirming in their clutch. The two muscular guards ignore me and continue to drag me along. "Where are we going?" I shout. Right then I see a huge research lab, surrounding me.

Doctors and nurses walk around, barely noticing me as they continue their work. They sit at long, grey tables, with telescopes and other equipment spread throughout the room. They all wear white coats with grey name tags. Every female doctor has their hair neatly tied up in a bun, and the men all carry around metal clipboards.

"Where am I?" I scream out, but no one looks around.

A doctor walks past us and I look at him. His eyes are grey and distant. He looks straight forwards, not even acknowledging I'm here. His mind seems to be elsewhere. The guards drag me over to another door a few feet away. I look around at the lab, noticing everyone seems to be under some kind of trance.

"Help!" I scream. No one even turns their head. My heartbeat is getting faster as my mind spins. "What's *wrong* with everyone?" I shout, causing the guards to tighten their grip on me.

A grey door opens on my left and a few surgeons walk out the room. They all wear masks with blood splattered across their aprons. I widen my eyes when the last one walks out holding a limp, young girl in his arms. I look at the girl and my heartbeat explodes.

"Leila?" I whisper. But I'm not even sure the words actually left my lips. My hands start to tremble at the sight of her thin bony frame, her lifeless arms and legs hanging from the doctor's firm hold.

"Leila!" I shout, trying to run towards her. The surgeon carries her out of the room, looking at me with fear in his eyes. "Leila! What have you *done* to her?" I continue screaming while attempting to squirm out of the guard's clutch, but it's no use. The surgeon immediately turns his back to me and carries her away, hurriedly running through a door on his right.

"*Leila!*" I scream again, trying my hardest to run after her, to save her. But the guard's grip bleeds into my arm, making me cry out in pain. There's no way I can help her now. There's no way I can escape this hell by myself — I'm too weak. But I will find a way to get to her.

Finally, the guards drag me into another hallway. I kick and fight with everything in me, screaming out to be let free. The guards continue to drag me, and my side starts to hurt so badly, it's keeping me at bay. A fire burns underneath my ribcage as they continue to walk over to a white door in front of us. Another few grey doors surround us, lining the hallway we now walk through. Each door has a touch-screen keypad by the side. When we get to the last one along the corridor, I try to run. But they only tighten their firm grip.

"What have you *done* to my sister?" I demand. But they push me into the little white room and close the door in my face.

Great. I punch the door in front of me and lean my head against the cool metal. *Why is Leila here? What are they doing to her? Are they going to do the same to me?* I hit the door once again and look around the room. A single bed sits in the corner of the eight-foot, square room. A small window lets the tiniest bit of light in, but it is wedged shut — probably to stop me from escaping.

Do each of the grey doors hold more prisoners? Why am I here? What do they want with me? I sit on the bed, holding my head in my hands. My mind goes towards the others. *What have they done to them? Is Zoe okay?*

I shut my eyes, thinking. I need to find Leila. I need to get us out of here. I just hope she's still alive. *Why am I in here and not with the others?* I don't understand. I sit back and lean my head against the cool metal wall.

The door suddenly opens and I whip my head around. A tall thin woman walks in wearing a glistening, white nurse's outfit. She holds a metal clipboard in her right hand. Her brown hair is pulled up neatly in a tight bun, with a few strands that had come loose hanging down, as if she's fighting against her perfect self. Something seems off about her, but when she looks up at me, my eyes immediately widen.

"*Mum?*" I ask, completely in shock. My throat is totally dry as I say the words. The woman looks up at me, but her eyes are grey and distant. She takes a seat next to me on the bed and looks through the paper on her clipboard. *She's alive. My mum's alive.*

"Mum!" I raise my voice. "Mum, it's me, Ella." I sit up, trying to get her attention. She looks at me as if I'm a stranger, as if I don't mean anything to her. She looks different, almost worn down. Her left cheek holds a dark purple bruise — her frame is weak and fragile, as if she could break at any moment. "Mum, what's *wrong* with you?" I try and shake her but she remains stiff like a robot. "Why is Leila here? Why are *you* here?" I ask, a small tear escaping down my pale cheek.

"You and your sister have something we need." She looks straight through me, as if she doesn't know who I am.

"What?" I ask, confused.

"You and your sister have something we need," she repeats.

"What do we have, Mum? *Please* tell me!" I feel like smacking her.

"You are very important to us." Her expression stays blank.

"Mum, what's *wrong* with you?" I try to shake her, but she stands up straight, glaring at me. Another tear rolls down my face. "We need to get out of here!" I say. But not even a flicker of emotion crosses her face.

"If you do not cooperate with our system, we will dispose of you." Her eyes flicker in annoyance.

"What?" I stand, ready to knock some sense into her. *What's happened to her? Why is she acting like she's in a trance?*

"Mum, please." I try to pull on her emotions, but she remains blank. "Mum, I know you're in there," I cry. All the lost pain within me pours into my pleas, as I relive the moment when I thought she had died, but she doesn't even blink. "*Mum!*" Salty tears are now streaming down my face.

"I think we're done here, doctor." A deep voice comes from behind me. A husky, mocking voice that causes me to immediately spin around to find the culprit responsible.

Mum ignores me and walks toward the door and out of the white room. As I watch my mum leave me, she turns the corner to reveal the last person I ever wanted to see: Derrick. He smirks, leaning against the doorframe.

"Welcome to The Society, Ella." His mouth curves up wickedly and I gulp.

Fuck.

ACKNOWLEDGEMENTS

Writing can be pretty lonely, especially at times when you are up so early writing down ideas from a dream that you've had, so I want to say a huge thank you to everyone involved in the making of this book. You guys are the reason Ella has come alive. You've made it happen.

Thank you to my parents, who have listened to me babbling on about my characters all day, everyday and have shown nothing but support.

My sister for getting me into writing in the first place, and my brother who introduced me to zombies – slightly obsessed now.

Another big thank you to all of my friends and family who have supported my writing from the very start, you all know who you are.

I want to say a huge thank you to Beth Hale, for putting up with my endless questions and emails, thank you for the amazing support and keeping me positive when I thought I was going to lose it.

Another thank you to Jill Weinstein for her amazing editing, truly a wonderful job! You've made Ella stronger and even more real than I could have ever imagined.

Thank you to Jessica Allain, her wonderful book cover, it made my whole entire year.

Thank you to Champagne formats for the wonderful job, creating the perfect structure and working extremely hard to create this beautiful book.

To all of my colleagues, readers and bloggers that supported me and made me realise there's nothing else I'd rather be doing, a great big thank you to you!

A thank you to Socks and Slippers for climbing all over my work and meowing constantly, reminding me that the real world is still waiting for some attention.

Also I want to say a huge thank you to everyone who has always believed in Ella and her adventures, she has finally come to life and I couldn't be happier.

14790827R00119

Printed in Great Britain
by Amazon.co.uk, Ltd.,
Marston Gate.